KNOWING YOU

Hearts of Ridgewood #1

Mia Jade

Trigger warnings: this book contains content that may be disturbing to some readers. It includes themes of abuse, mental health struggles, drug and alcohol abuse, domestic violence, and graphic depictions of violence and distressing situations. Reader discretion is strongly advised.

For my mother, who stood by me in the worst of times and made this book possible; and for the girls who spent their entire lives carrying the weight of the world on their shoulders.

AUTHOR'S NOTE

Knowing You is the first book for Archie and Savannah, and the first book overall. Some scenes may be disturbing or upsetting, and I strongly advise you to put your mental health first.

Writing Knowing You has been a wonderful journey that took me places I never expected to go. So, for anybody who has been torn between what they want and what they fear, this one's for you.

Chapter one

February 2nd 2004

SAVANNAH

I was eleven years old when I first realised the only real problem in my life was me. While I'd had a lot of pain forced upon me, it seemed obvious that I was the common factor.

To say that everyone else had hurt me in unimaginable ways may be true, but I couldn't simply blame the people around me for the twisted ways my brain worked. It wasn't only about that. It was the way I allowed it to sink into my bones and twist the way I saw everything, including myself.

It had to be me. I had to be the problem.

That was the conclusion I'd come to. It wasn't a good one, but it was honest.

Life had never played fair. Not with me. It was a disappointment, and a cruel one at that. It felt like the universe had thrown its worst hand at me and expected me to keep my smile bright until the end.

Now, at fifteen, not much had changed.

Maybe that was just how the world worked.

Maybe some people were born lucky, and others were born... me. Maybe some people were handed love, and others were handed survival.

I got survival.

But I'd gotten good at living with it. At surviving in the grey space between what I showed, and what I truly felt.

And if I had to blame one person for my ways of surviving, there would be no question.

Michael Grey.

My father.

My house should have been the first place I learned safety and love. But that wasn't the life I was born into. Instead, I learned of hate, violence and fear.

I learned to flinch earlier than laugh. How to listen for footsteps like they were warnings.

I think being born into a family with no love to give changes people, and turns them into somebody they never would have been otherwise.

I think it changed me.

But I also had a problem with focusing on the sadness inside of my soul rather than the happiness I'd found outside of it.

Truly, it wasn't all bad.

There were people. Beautiful, stubborn people who hadn't given up on me, even in the hardest of times.

I had Liv and Josie who saved me a seat in every room, who never made me question whether I was wanted. Izzie, with sharp edges that cut anybody who got too close, but still tried her hardest to let me all the way in.

Even the boys. Theo, Danny and Billy. Danny, being Izzie's brother, had never hesitated to invite me to his childhood birthday parties or offer to hang out with me when the girls were out sick. While I never took him up on those offers, I appreciated the thought behind it.

Theo was Liv's best friend, and despite his best efforts of coping with humour and acting above feelings, he was truly lovely underneath the mask.

Even Billy, who was strangely quiet, had been wonderful to me throughout our years at school. Izzie and Billy had a very complicated relationship, to say the least.

Then there was Marlee.

She was gone now. Dead.

It hurt to even think of her.

Marlee was the kind of friend you could never take for granted. Impossibly beautiful, loud, and unafraid of the world.

Well, that was until the world showed her its claws.

I hated the way I felt when I thought about her. It felt selfish, like I was angry at her for leaving me behind. But I wasn't angry at her. Not in the slightest. I was angry at the world for taking her away from me. For making her believe her time was over, when that couldn't have been the truth.

I couldn't stop thinking about how wrong it was. How unfair.

It was last year. Ninth grade. She hadn't turned fifteen yet, damn it. There was no way some bigger force needed her more than we did.

It hurt knowing I had to go back today.

We'd done the remainder of last year after her death, but we'd all taken so much time off. The days I did attend had all faded into an endless blur of pain and grief, so this was the first time I'd be going back with a relatively clear mind.

That's why Izzie was so angry.

They were the closest.

She'd watched it happen.

If I were her, I would have hated the universe too. Her best friend was taken from this life, and she witnessed it. She heard the sounds. Saw the air leave her lungs. The light leaving her eyes.

I hated when people labeled her as angry as if she didn't have every reason to be.

If anybody had a reason to be angry, it was Izzie Harris.

But I could never let those thoughts linger for very long.

If I let them stay, I'd spiral. Again.

I wasn't ready for this year. But I had to be. Because no one else would do it for me.

I'd learned a long time ago that nobody was coming to save me. That if I didn't step out of my shell and speak every now and then, there was no way of escaping the pain that consumed me.

I either saved myself, or stayed drowning forever.

Neither of those options sounded very easy, but what else was I supposed to do?

Staring into the shattered mirror by my window, I saw the face that had been the subject of too many unwanted thoughts. Grey eyes that had lost any semblance of toughness over the years. Eyes that had witnessed too much to remain innocent.

My brown waves had finally grown out, now long enough to brush the bottom of my chest. The strands framed my face in a way that made me look somehow less vulnerable, but I knew better. No amount of messy waves or pale skin dotted with freckles would ever change the truth: I was broken, and regardless of how hard I tried to hide that fact, I knew everyone could see it.

I had curves now, too. Not enough to make me feel like I was anything but an afterthought in this world that wanted to break me, but enough to get commented on. Enough to remind me that I was growing up when Marlee couldn't.

I didn't like it. I didn't like the attention, or the comments, or the stares that lingered just a little too long.

I liked being invisible.

Invisibility was safe.

It kept me alive.

I tugged the navy blue blazer over the yellow-and-blue checkered dress that clung too tightly to my skin, feeling all wrong. Too stiff. These were colours I'd learned to survive in, not thrive. Despite the fancy buildings and expensive decorations, Ridgewood wasn't a nice place.

Because nobody brought Marlee the help she needed.

I sighed, draping my bag on top. I wasn't ready in the slightest. But I had to be. For them.

My brothers.

My friends who stuck by me through it all.

I had to be strong for them.

Because otherwise? There would be no strength left.

Because if I didn't hold everything together, there was no one else who would.

Maybe even for my mother. But God, how I hated her some days. She was the only person with the ability to get us out of this house. But she never would. She'd never help us in the way we needed her to. I loved her. Truly, I did. I knew she loved us too, but she'd sure been horrible at showing it all these years. The reason behind that being the monster she married.

My father.

He was a wreck. A drunk. A man who made promises with his hands, only to break them with fists. I wasn't afraid of him anymore, not really. At least I wanted to stop being afraid. But I was tired. I was so damn tired of waiting for him to get better, or even to get worse.

I was six years old the last time I saw him sober. He smiled at me that day, *really* smiled, and I think, as naive as it was, I believed in it. In him.

But those fleeting moments were just a cruel illusion, because it didn't take long until the next fight.

I took one last glance in the mirror, smoothing down the blue and yellow dress that sat awkwardly beneath the blazer. This uniform was awfully unflattering.

I pulled open my bedroom door, the creaking sound echoing through the house like it always did in the morning.

Our small, double story house still smelled faintly of cigarettes and whiskey, but that wasn't anything out of the usual.

I slowly made my way down the stairs, avoiding the steps that I *knew* would creak.

My oldest brother, Jayden, was already in the kitchen, sitting at the cracked table with a coffee in hand. He was swirling it in these slow, deliberate movements that told me he was desperately willing himself not to fall apart.

I hated how much I understood.

"Dad's already gone," he muttered, his voice flat, devoid of the anger that I knew he was hiding. "Out at the bar again. I'd say he's not coming back 'till after midnight, if we're lucky."

I swallowed hard, not trusting myself to speak. Jayden wasn't angry anymore. Not like he used to be. And that scared me more than his anger had. Now? He was just… numb. A shell of a human.

He used to get angry. He would throw things or punch holes in the wall when it became too much to handle. But now? He did exactly this.

Just sipped his coffee and pretended everything was fine.

Jayden was eighteen this year.

If he wanted to, he could leave in July.

No questions, no control.

But I knew he wouldn't.

He would never willingly leave us in this house alone, even though it killed him to stay.

I hated that he felt the need to do that.

His only consolation was his girlfriend, Caroline Bailey. The two of them had been dating on and off for years, and I knew he was utterly in love with her. Consumed by her.

I loved that he had that.

I envied it, too.

Me? Being in a relationship was the last thing I wanted. I couldn't deal with the weight of another person relying on me when I could barely rely on myself.

Jayden and I came from the same house, but we were cut from different cloth.

Besides the obvious things, his blonde hair and sharp, hazel eyes in contrast to my features, we had merely one similarity.

He fought. I folded.

He let people in. I slammed every door shut.

He looked for a way out.

I looked for a way to disappear.

It was always humorous to me, the way two people could lead the same childhood yet turn out as two entirely different people.

Malcolm sat down at the table then, dragging me away from my thoughts. He had a cheap magazine in his small hands, fingers tracing the pages like they were a map to someplace else. Someplace better.

Malcolm was practically the same as Jayden at twelve. Same looks, same personality. His face was still innocent, and we'd shielded him from a lot of it, but that wasn't to say he thought we lived a normal life.

I knew he'd get it soon enough. After all, you can shield kids from a war as long as you like, but you can't hide the fact they're growing up in the middle of one.

Jayden and I were living proof of that.

Leo was on the floor, playing with some broken toy I couldn't even recognize anymore. He looked up at me with wide, trusting eyes, and it almost hurt to look at him. He was young enough to stay protected now, but he'd be ten in a few months. For me and Jayden, ten years old was where it all went wrong.

I'd do anything in my power to put an end to that cycle.

I poured myself a glass of water, trying to avoid looking at Jayden. I didn't miss it. The way his brown eyes scanned my body for bruises before he met my eyes, the way he monitored the breathing in my parents' room like a soldier on patrol.

"Do you need me to drop you off?" Jayden finally asked, his voice almost too calm, as though he didn't want to break the fragile silence that hung between us.

I shook my head, throat tight. "Liv's picking me up."

He raised an eyebrow. "Liv's fifteen."

"You were fourteen."

A small chuckle escaped his lips, causing me to grin. "Alright, Savvy. Just... don't die."

"Right." I gave a small smile, turning to leave the kitchen.

As I approached the front door, his rough voice called after me. "You'll do great, savvy. You...you look lovely."

I didn't respond. I couldn't.

With that, I was stepping back into the real world. The one I'd spent the entire summer hiding from.

"Sav!" Liv called, poking her head out the window. Her blonde curls were thrown into a messy bun, flyways escaping in every direction, but it didn't matter. Liv could show up in pyjamas and bed-hair and still look like she stepped right out of a fairytale. "You're never on time."

I groaned, sliding into the passenger seat. "I'm sorry!"

She glared at me while turning the car on, but there was a smile in her voice. "Do you have some sort of personal vendetta against punctuality?"

I laughed. Like, really laughed.

Liv was the only one able to stop me caving in on myself.

She was the only one that had pulled me out of my bubble wrap.

"You're lucky I love you," she said, flicking on her blinker with unnecessary aggression.

I grinned, buckling my seatbelt. "You're legally obligated. Best friend code."

She rolled her eyes but leaned over to squeeze my hand before pulling out onto the main road.

"Can I convince you to join cheer this year?" Liv asked, green eyes full of hope.

"Lower your dreams," I laughed, but it went deeper than that.

I didn't have any form of control over my life. Maybe one day, but not yet.

I wasn't the sort of girl who could show up. The type of girl to be a cheerleader. I wasn't carefree like everyone else.

"Fine," she sighed dramatically. "I'll try again later in the year."

I smiled along, but my attention was elsewhere.

I was staring at the middle seat in the back, where Marlee used to sit. The seat that would forever be empty in her absence.

She'd left a hole in our hearts, and she didn't even know it.

But I couldn't dwell on it. I couldn't let the thoughts in, or I'd spiral. Again.

I needed to allow myself peace.

At least that.

That's why I was still here.

Still trying, against all odds.

The music played low, something old and unknown, the kind of thing Marlee would've made fun of and then secretly downloaded on her Ipod.

I swallowed hard, forcing my eyes back to the road.

"You okay?" Liv asked, her voice too soft. She didn't look at me. She knew better. If she looked at me, she wouldn't miss it. She'd see all of the pain, all the years of lies. So she chose not to on mornings like these.

"Yeah," I lied. "Just tired."

She didn't call me out on it. She never did.

"You miss her today," she said quietly.

It wasn't a question.

I nodded. "I miss her every day."

"I know," she whispered, a sad smile appearing on her face. "We all do."

We didn't talk after that. There wasn't much else to say.

Our most chattery friend was gone.

By the time we pulled into the school parking lot, the sun had risen just enough to make the building look less intimidating. The new year sevens piled in, looking happy enough that today almost felt like a fresh start for me, too.

Almost.

"You ready?" she asked, hand still on the key.

"No," I answered honestly. "But I'm going anyway."

She smiled softly. "That's my girl."

I glanced around, noticing how much had changed over the summer.

It was the same false, rich school it had always been, but it seemed emptier this year. Less lively.

We all knew why that was.

Chapter two

February 2nd 2004

SAVANNAH

I hated walking through the hallways when my friends were nowhere to be seen.

It wasn't safe. Not at all.

Some naive part of me wanted to believe that today would be different. That the laughter would stop and I could just *breathe.*

But I'd stopped believing in miracles a long time ago.

"Hey," a familiar voice called, sharp and falsely sweet all at once. "How's the friend doing? Still dead?"

I froze. Her perfume hit me all at once, and for a moment, I could have mistaken it for Marlee's. That cheap vanilla and coconut scent I remembered so well.

But these girls weren't gentle or sweet like Marlee.

I didn't need to turn to know it was them. Casey, Tahlia, and whoever their friends were that fed off cruelty.

"Wait," Casey added, mockingly thoughtful. "Maybe Marlee killed herself to get away from *you.*"

Tahlia's bitter laugh sliced the air. "Maybe the wrong friend died."

I didn't say anything.

I couldn't.

I could barely breathe.

Walk away, Savannah.

Walk. Away.

Don't you dare cry!

But my feet wouldn't move. They were stuck in place.

By now, I should have been strong enough to fight back. I'd endured enough cruel words and sharp looks from these girls, but it didn't matter.

I couldn't bring myself to be confrontational.

It felt mean.

I wanted to stay kind.

Maybe I did deserve this from them. If I'd noticed the signs from Marlee sooner, I could have been the one to keep her there. Maybe I did notice and wanted to give her space. How could I deserve kindness if mine wasn't strong enough to keep her alive?

"I mean, if I had to spend everyday with you, I'd off myself too," another girl continued, earning a chorus of laughter from the group.

Tahlia rolled her eyes, preparing to speak again, but that's when another voice came through.

A voice that I could almost recognise.

"Say that again."

Everything froze.

The air. The cruelty. The laughter.

I turned my head slowly. Carefully.

Archie Bennett.

Basketball captain. Everyone's favorite *everything*. He had that effortless charm that made every guy want to be him, and every girl want to be *with* him.

6'4, with dark brown hair and those sharp green eyes that felt like they could cut right through me.

He was standing a few feet away, a hard expression on his face.

Why was he defending *me?*

He barely knew me.

"Relax," Casey laughed, but she took a careful step backwards. She knew as well as I did that Archie Bennett had more power than her. "It was a joke."

Archie raised an eyebrow, stepping closer. His movement wasn't aggressive, but it had an air of authority that I couldn't ignore.

I knew he wouldn't lay a hand on either of the girls, but he knew he was in control of the situation. He was popular, but I never saw the boy as cruel.

Still, he stood there, unwavering, and I could tell each of the girls respected, or feared him, because they all took another step back.

"You're making *jokes* about a girl who's not even here to defend herself?"

Tahlia scoffed. "We were-"

"No," Archie interrupted firmly. "The lot of you hide behind cruelty because you're too scared to admit that you played a huge part in Marlee McGovern's death. Now, you'll stay the fuck away from Savannah from now on. Got that?"

"Got it." Tahlia scoffed, rolling her eyes. "Come on, girls."

Watching them walk away, I blinked back the tears that threatened to spill.

Archie's expression softened as he turned to look at me. "Are you okay?"

I nodded, but my eyes gave it all away.

Blowing out a shaky breath, he asked, "Do you wanna get out of here for a minute?"

I blinked, confused, wondering if I had heard him right. He wanted to get out of here? With *me?*

My heart did this stupid thing where it skipped, and I immediately regretted it.

No, this wasn't supposed to happen.

Archie was not someone I could trust, someone I could get attached to. I had spent years building walls around my heart, and now this boy was threatening to knock them down with one stupid question.

Damn it, Savannah.

You're smarter than this!

"With you?" I heard myself ask, still confused.

A small chuckle escaped his full lips. "Yeah. With me."

"I don't know if…" I trailed off, finally meeting his gaze. "Okay then."

Suddenly, it felt like maybe I wasn't the problem at all.

Before I could procrastinate any further, I was walking along the outdoor basketball courts with Archie Bennett.

The person I would have least expected.

"Don't listen to them," he said roughly, taking a seat on the wooden bench along the year ten building. "They're projecting."

That was easier said than done.

Those girls were the only ones who dared to speak her name.

Nobody else was stupid, or brave enough.

Not after her mother, Lila McGovern, had threatened multiple lawsuits.

I didn't even blame her. Marlee was an only child, and they had a very close bond. Looking back, I was utterly jealous of their relationship. But now? It felt stupid to think I envied something that small. Because at least she was *alive* to have that relationship.

That wasn't the case anymore.

I wasn't sure how to accept that.

Cutting through the tension, Archie changed the subject. Thankfully.

"You're Olivia Mallory's best friend," he stated, clearly aware of the answer as he gestured for me to take a seat. "Savannah Grey?"

With a slow, careful nod, I joined him on the bench, leaving an appropriate distance between us.

Archie Bennett wasn't somebody I could risk getting infatuated with.

I wasn't one of those girls.

He didn't do relationships. That was a widely known fact.

Me? I wasn't exactly the sort of girl to jump at the chance of a one night stand with the golden boy of Ridgewood.

Of course, the fact that I'd never even kissed anybody played a big part in that.

God, I shouldn't have even been thinking about him like that.

But my heart was already beating too fast, a flush creeping up my neck before I could stop it.

"Yeah," I finally replied.

"You were…" He hesitated, green eyes searching my face. "Were you there the night Marlee…"

"No," I cut him off, unwilling to hear the end of that sentence. "That was Izzie."

"Danny's baby sister?" He raised a brow. "Fuck. He never told me that."

"She probably asked him not to speak about it." Offering him a polite smile, I said, "You don't need to sit with me, you know?"

"I know," He chuckled quietly, stretching his arms above his head, muscles flexing with the movement. "But I'm not that much of a dick."

I shouldn't have been sitting with him.

My whole life, I'd never found interest in anyone. But his dark green eyes locked on mine, and I just…There was a strange sense of something I'd almost forgotten existed. Hope.

In my experience, hope was only ever dangerous.

And I needed to get far, far away from this boy.

He wasn't supposed to be sweet. He was supposed to laugh with the rest of them and avoid girls like me.

But maybe I wasn't the only one good at wearing a mask.

"I have to go," I told him, suddenly standing up. "Um, thanks for helping me today."

He nodded slowly, like maybe he wanted me to stay.

But I was reading too much into it.

Archie Bennett was *not* for me.

So I turned around, instantly walking in the opposite direction.

"Hey Sav?" He called, causing me to turn around. "I'll be seeing you."

I hesitated before plastering on a very practiced smile. "Maybe you will."

I turned. Quicker this time. The moment my back was to him, my smile disappeared, and the tall, polished buildings of Ridgewood came into my view.

All I could do was remind myself of this: nothing changes.

That was one thing I knew for a fact.

Thought I knew.

Because I was wrong.
I was so very wrong.

Chapter three

February 6th 2004

ARCHIE

Training was brutal, and we were only halfway through the hour.

But I didn't care.

Training days were *good* days.

The court was to me what a church must be for christians. *My* place. My *sanctuary*

In the gym, nothing mattered other than the next shot and the next sprint that had my legs threatening to give out.

Basketball came easy to me. Like breathing. Or swimming. Or riding a bike.

That wasn't to say it was never hard. I'd given my blood, sweat, and fucking tears for the game.

And I had no regrets. It was worth it.

Because I was the best on the team. The guys knew it, Coach knew it. The whole of Ridgewood knew it.

I knew that was an arrogant thing to say, but I'd worked for it. My whole life was about the game, and it was something nobody could take. It was just for *me*.

"Bennett!" Theo called, appearing behind me in a way that always fucking creeped me out.

"Hi," I replied dryly to my best friend, throwing my third ball through the hoop.

Swish.

Training was by far the highlight of my day, every day.

Even though it meant putting up with Theo.

"Look at that girl, man." Theo shook his head in disbelief, practically drooling at the sight of Olivia Mallory in her cheer uniform.

His best friend, must I add.

The two of them had been best friends since prep. Back then, he'd pretended she meant the same as the rest of the girls. Purely platonic. But now? He looked at that girl like she hung the fucking stars.

"So," I started, carefully searching his blue eyes. "Why are ya still friends?"

"Because he's a dickhead," Billy chimed in, appearing out of nowhere. "He's too afraid to acknowledge the fact you *don't* drool at the sight of your *friend.*"

"How very fucking insightful of you," Theo deadpanned.

I sighed, ready to put out yet another fire between the two of them before it started. "Shut it down."

Those two couldn't get along for the fucking life of them. I mean, they were close when they wanted to be. But they could also rip each other's throats out just as well.

Billy Hastings and Danny Harris were the only guys other than Theo who I truly considered my friends.

There were a million fuckers around here that had attempted to form a friendship with me, but it wasn't worth it.

I didn't need a list of friends.

I had three, and that was more than enough.

More than that would only enhance the stress.

That didn't mean I hadn't regretted not branching out at times.

Last year more than ever.

When Izzie had became angry and Danny, as well as Billy, needed my help with her, I had no fucking clue what to tell them.

I think the sudden change had something to do with Marlee.

I wouldn't know.

I hadn't been there.

Hadn't *been there* for any of them, really.

All three of my friends' were close with the girls. That didn't mean I had an obligation to be. At least, that's what I told myself.

But now?

I felt like a fucking asshole.

I missed it.

All of it.

I hadn't even known Marlee beyond the way the boys used to talk about her. This bright, reckless girl who was bound to change the world someday.

And now she was just...a story.

One I hadn't bothered listening to until it was too late.

I bloody hated the way people around here spoke her name. Like she was the *gossip* of the week.

Christ, I figured it was human decency to put some respect on the girl's name. But nope. No one around here got that fucking memo.

I wiped my forehead with the back of my hand and jogged back into the drill.

Work harder.

Think less.

That was the deal.

It had always been the deal, especially after everything with my dad.

Feeling things only got you hurt.

Caring only slowed you down.

It was the same with girls.

Fun for a night, a few weeks if they were lucky, but never anything more.

Never anyone I actually thought about when they weren't standing right in front of me.

Until Monday.

Until *her.*

The random girl I'd stepped in for. I didn't even know her name at first. It took me a while to recognise her as Olivia's best friend.

I saw a girl being harassed, and figured it would be a dick move to walk straight past when I *knew* I could help.

Her gentle voice was still in my head, that achingly vulnerable tone, the pink flush on her cheeks making my chest feel too tight.

And the worst part?

I couldn't stop thinking about it.

About *her.*

About how none of it made sense.

I was *bloody confused* and I hated it.

Whatever bizarre effect this girl had on my mind wasn't normal. Not for me.

I didn't like it.

Not. At. All.

Someone slammed into me mid-drill and I stumbled, blinking hard, trying to shove it all out of my head.

Theo chuckled, clapping me on the shoulder. "You good, bud?"

I gritted my teeth and nodded, forcing my brain back to the game.

Back to the only place where I knew the rules.

Because whatever the hell this girl was doing to my mind didn't align with the rules I'd set. Not at all.

The guys started tossing the ball around five minutes later like they had all the time in the world. Maybe they did, but I sure as hell didn't. I'd always known basketball was my future. My purpose. My ticket out.

Billy started making half-assed attempts at shooting hoops from the corner, missing every single time. He always did that. Pretended not to care. But come game day? He was a fucking beast. Six foot something with broad shoulders, dark brown hair and those sharp, hazel eyes that made him look permanently pissed off. He wasn't, though.

After five years of friendship, you'd think I'd have known more about the guy. But he was the most closed-off person I'd met in my sixteen years. What I did know was that he'd been through a whole load of shit.

Still, he was the calmest of us all. It had always been that way.

"Hastings!" Danny called, blonde hair falling into his face as he mindlessly scrolled through his phone. "Can you call my psycho of a fucking twin?"

Billy groaned, shoulders visibly tensing. "Don't be a dick," he muttered beneath his breath. "On it."

Danny had stopped trying when it came to Izzie. He loved the girl, that much was clear, but he'd given up on trying to fix her. I couldn't blame him. She brought more bad into his life than good.

Billy didn't care, though.

Christ, Izzie Harris could have stuck a knife through his throat and he'd still spend his last breaths making sure she was okay.

But Danny always had some sort of strange, careless attitude about him. Right now, he was off to the sidelines, not even pretending to try. He was good. Really good. If basketball meant to him what it did the rest of us, he would have been a fucking star. But we all knew it'd never be more than a hobby for him.

The only real intensity in Danny came out when he was arguing with Izzie. Their relationship was…volcanic, to say the least.

Theo threw the ball then, missing my face by a half centimeter, pissing me off for the seventh time this morning.

"You alright?"

I glared at him. "How the fuck are you still on the team?"

"You wound me." His grin stretched wider. "Well, if I don't make it on the court I think I'd be a bloody wonderful cheerleader."

"You'd make billions," I said, deadpan.

I truly questioned our friendship. Like, really often. He *did* have the skills. He was just too busy... watching the cheerleaders. One cheerleader, I should say.

I never knew what was going on between the two of them, but I did know his feelings for the girl were real.

He could have any girl he wanted. Truly. And I wouldn't say that about anyone else. Not even myself. Tall, with a mop of blonde curls that never looked messy on him, and those ridiculous blue eyes that only lit up when Olivia was around.

There was nobody else for him.

But I wasn't sure he'd even come to terms with his own feelings yet, let alone hers.

"Alright boys, let's show up or shut up," Coach barked, dragging me back into the present. "I've got myself some fine players, so the doors wide open for anybody who doesn't care enough to get on the court." His wrinkly face crinkled further as he glared at Danny.

"Got it, Coach," Danny replied, embarrassment clear in his blue eyes.

Theo's gaze shifted past Coach, of course, and directly to the sidelines.

"Callahan!" Coach shouted. "Quit eyeing the blonde and get your head in the game."

Theo looked back almost immediately, chuckling awkwardly. "Sorry Coach."

I didn't need to look to know it was Olivia.

It was *only* ever Olivia for him.

Coach began shouting at him again, but I didn't care.

Because *she* just walked in.

Savannah Grey.

She showed up to watch Josie and Olivia cheer every Friday, but I'd never noticed her until now. Not really.

Lately, I couldn't focus on anything other than that certain pair of grey eyes. Her light brown waves were smooth and silky, thrown into a low ponytail, something I couldn't quite tear my eyes away from.

It was fucking pathetic.

I hadn't even spoken to the girl since that day in the hall.

There were a million other girls in Ridgewood who would gladly jump at the chance to date me. Actually, many of them were stupid enough to try.

Then, there was the fact that I had a strict no-girlfriend policy.

I shouldn't have even been having thoughts of girlfriends. I couldn't bend that rule for a girl I knew nothing about.

There was a whole group of cheerleaders in front of her, half of which I'd already messed around with, but I didn't care. I didn't want to look at them.

But that wasn't my problem.

Problem was, it wasn't purely physical with her like it was with every other girl.

That wasn't to say I hadn't been admiring her body or the fact that for a girl only 5 '4, she had incredibly long legs, because that would be a lie. She was attractive, and I appreciated that.

But for the first time in my life, that wasn't *all*.

I wanted to know *her*, damn it.

It wasn't about what was beneath the clothes. It was about what was in her *heart* and *mind*. I wanted to know what her favourite song was and why she hid herself from the world.

I'd never given two fucks about that with anybody else.

I hadn't defended her that day for no reason. I hadn't sat with her simply to make her feel better, even if that's what I told myself.

I did both of those things because *I* genuinely wanted to.

I didn't know why. There was nothing big. It was almost like all I had to do was speak to the girl one time, and just like that, nothing mattered.

Fuck, I hated feelings.

"Bennett." Coach's rough voice snapped me out of whatever haze I'd allowed myself to fall into. "Take a break."

"It's training." I lifted an eyebrow, a smile playing on my lips. "We don't do breaks."

"Now we do." An oddly large smirk appeared on his face as he pulled me toward the bench.

Still, I sat down without hesitation. Nobody ignored Coach Holloway's orders. Not unless they had a death wish.

Whistles blew again, and everybody else was back on the court.

"Archer." Coach's voice softened once it was just the two of us. I visibly cringed at the use of my full name. It made it feel too serious. "How ya holdin' up, kid?"

I winced in discomfort. "Coach, we don't have to do the whole-"

"Nonsense," he interrupted, clapping a wrinkled hand on my shoulder. "You've got a whole heap of demons running around in that head of yours, and I'm not about to ignore 'em. I'm not about to let you ignore 'em, either. Now, like it or not, you're a son to me. That means I *do* have to check in."

I swallowed hard, willing myself to keep the hard exterior in front of the one man who always showed up for me. "Thanks Coach."

He gave me a supportive wink before turning to yell at one of my teammates, but I wasn't listening. His words went directly to my head. They always did.

Coach Holloway had stepped up when nobody else did. Well, when nobody else could.

My dad and little sister died two years before Marlee, and he'd been the one to show up consistently. Even when I insisted I was fine. *Especially* when I insisted I was fine.

It started with extra drills and one-on-one training sessions, but somewhere along the way, he became somebody I could trust. Someone who truly gave a shit. Maybe that meant more than I cared to admit.

Yeah, feelings sucked.

I thought about my sister, Elsie, for a second. How she would have laughed her head off hearing about this. How she would've teased me for being a goner after five bloody minutes.

Miss you, I thought, throat tight. *Miss you every day.*

Savannah caught my eye from the wooden bleachers again, her mouth twitching into something that could have been a smile if she didn't look so hauntingly sad.

Yeah, I had a feeling this wasn't the last time I'd be seeing her.

Chapter four

February 13th 2004

SAVANNAH

The house had already started falling apart before I even made it down the stairs.

Dad's sharp voice was shaking the walls, causing the framed 'family' photos to fall and shatter.

Mum was as hopeless as ever. Sitting in the corner of the kitchen, she hid her face behind her hands and sobbed, like maybe that was the best way to disappear. Like if she hid and pretended this was a dream, maybe it would become one.

Jayden was standing between Dad and our three younger brothers, arms spread wide, his whole body tense like he could actually stop it all.

I didn't flinch when something smashed against the wall. I just gripped the railing tighter, even though my hands were already trembling, and forced myself to keep moving. I was the second oldest. The only girl. I had to be brave. I had to be.

Right on cue, my father launched himself at me. I was his least favourite child, and he'd never been ashamed to admit that.

He'd said it in multiple birthday speeches.

Multiple parties.

In all honesty, I wasn't sure how nobody had caught on to the fact that my house was far from normal.

Except Liv.

She didn't know the extent of the abuse, but she knew, without a doubt, that life had never been kind to me.

His willingness to admit his hatred for me was my reason for not being surprised as his calloused fist met my cheek, knocking my body to the cold, hard tiles.

There was a voice in my head, begging, screaming, clawing at me to hit him back. To fight. To scream. Hell, just to move. But I didn't. Not because I forgave him or believed he deserved any kindness, but I knew how much worse that would make it.

"Get the fuck off her!" Jayden roared, wasting no time. He was over in an instant, using all his strength to rip my father away from my body.

"What ya gonna do 'bout it, boy?" My father laughed, that familiar, predatory sound that still haunted my dreams. "Think you're stronger than me?"

"I think I'll do everything I can to keep you the fuck away from her." His voice raised to something more dangerous, matching my fathers. "I'm not a defenceless teenage girl, and I'm not a child. Fight somebody your own size."

"You're fucking askin' for it, aren't ya?" My father snapped, knocking my older brother right to the ground.

The harsh sound of his body hitting the tiles echoed throughout the kitchen, sending another wave of fear right through me.

My mother's lifeless brown eyes were fixed on the ground. Not a glance spared for me, for Jayden. Not even for the boys clinging to each other on the couch.

I remember being eight years old, and standing in front of my mum after another of my dad's outbursts. While they weren't as violent back then, it was enough. I asked her why she never stopped him from hurting us. She looked me dead in the eye and said, "Because I can't." That was the day I stopped asking.

Conflicted, I turned my gaze to the boys. Malcolm's hands were already balled into fists, anger radiating from him. Leo was holding our baby brother, Aidan, close, already a protector at nine years old.

Fuck.

I hated being unable to help these situations.

This is why, I had to remind myself. *This is why you need to stay away from Archie Bennett.*

Before my eyes, Malcolm rose from the couch and hurried over to my father who was still on top of Jayden.

"Get. Off. Him!"

"Mal," Jayden warned, struggling beneath our fathers weight. "It's okay."

"No the fuck it's not!" He snapped, attempting to shove our father off. Of course, he wasn't strong enough. None of us were.

The look in his chocolate brown eyes, somewhere between angry and petrified, caused a familiar ache to bloom in my chest. He looked more and more like Jayden every bloody day.

That wasn't a bad thing, I suppose.

But all four of my brothers had the genes of both of our parents.

That meant the boys would follow in Jayden's footsteps and have to put up with the 'you look exactly like your father' speeches that I knew shattered his heart.

I was the only one who never faced those issues.

Though, it never quite made sense, how different I looked in comparison to the rest of my family.

Jayden managed to escape our father's grip, shoving him to the ground, wiping the blood dripping from the corners of his mouth. "Had your fun, dad?" He asked, voice dripping with sarcasm and bitterness.

Dad scoffed, casually heading for his bedroom.

Like nothing happened.

Like nothing had *ever* happened.

Mum trailed after him like a lost puppy, never stopping to check on any one of us.

She loved us. She did. But I was growing tired of convincing myself of that fact every day.

She was terrified of that man. I understood that better than anybody, but that didn't make it fair.

Whatever dedication and twisted form of 'love', she thought she had for him, would always come above her love for us.

The love that *should* have been stronger.

"Savvy," Jayden muttered from the floor, wiping the blood from the corners of his mouth. "Would ya take the boys up to Caroline so I can clean this shit up?"

"Do you need help?" I heard myself ask.

"Yeah, help by getting them upstairs."

I didn't hesitate. "Let's go, boys," I urged, voice low and broken.

I was never able to keep it together in the way Jayden could.

I picked Aidan up in my arms, heading straight for the stairs. Malcolm and Leo followed closely behind, both shaken up.

I hated when they got caught up in the aggression.

Usually, we got lucky and it was only Jayden & I downstairs when this level of violence occurred.

Tonight…we didn't get lucky.

I hated it for them because I knew we couldn't keep this from them.

After all, we could try to shield kids from a war for as long as we liked, but we couldn't hide the fact that they were growing up in the middle of one.

Jayden and I were living proof of that.

Once we reached the top of the stairs, I crouched down to my brothers' levels. "Are you okay?"

Leo nodded. Then shook his head.

I pulled him in for a tight hug, holding him and Aidan impossibly close.

"I'm scared," Leo choked out, sniffling against my shoulder.

"I know, buddy." My eyes flickered up to meet Malcolm's. Against his best attempts at hiding it, fear radiated from him like a strong perfume. I pulled him into my arms. "I know."

"Can we see Ca-line?" Leo asked, wiping his eyes as he pulled away from the hug.

"Her name's Caroline, dipshit," Malcolm corrected sarcastically.

I huffed a laugh, glad to see that Malcolm was still himself. "Course we can, bud."

I directed my brothers' to the end of the hall, stopping once we reached Jayden's room.

The door was already open, Caroline perched on the end of his queen-sized bed, hands wrung nervously together in her lap.

"Shit," she said beneath her breath, instantly moving toward us. "Are you okay?"

Lined up against the wall like crime suspects, each of us nodded, and I almost could have laughed at how easily we lied.

Caroline moved for me first, blonde hair falling into her face. "I'm so sorry, Savvy."

"It's okay," I mumbled, so quiet that it sounded unconvincing even to me.

She nodded, pulling me into her tight embrace.

Caroline Bailey truly was our saving grace. She'd been dating Jayden on and off for years

now, and she'd picked up the broken pieces of
our family.

She was the only one outside of our family
who knew the true extent of the abuse we'd
endured since the day Jayden was born.

Caroline moved for the boys next, hugging
each of them. Her hazel eyes shone with
sympathy and devastation as she did, but she
remained calm. She had an amazing ability to
keep the peace. Always had.

"Do you need a break?" She gave me a sad,
maybe even pitiful smile. "I can watch them.
Jayden will be up soon if you wanna go
somewhere else."

I wanted to decline her offer.

I wanted to pretend I was strong enough to
deal with this.

So badly.

But I couldn't.

Not tonight.

"If you don't mind?" I anxiously pressed my
teeth into my bottom lip. "I might go to Liv's if
that's…um, if that's okay?"

"Of course." She nodded, an affectionate
look on her face despite the circumstances. "Try
to…" She hesitated. "Try to have a good night,
okay?"

Unsure, I simply nodded.

✦

After a ten minute walk in the pouring rain, I finally arrived on Liv's impressive front porch.

Reaching up with a trembling hand, I knocked quietly.

I knew Liv would welcome me with open arms, and I knew that she would never question my random arrivals if it was clear I wasn't going to speak about it.

But I was gutted.

I'd been numb to a lot of my fathers outbreaks recently, but watching my little brothers grow up and learn the routine of violence like a school bell shattered me.

They didn't deserve that.

Neither had I, I realized.

But here I was.

"Hey!" Liv greeted, her smile almost too bright. She didn't comment on the way my sleeves were deliberately tucked in, or the bruised knuckles. She never did.

I loved her for that.

Plastering on a smile that wasn't even close to meeting my eyes, I took a careful step inside.

Liv's house was massive, and it only surprised me more each time I came. It was always messy, though. I wasn't one to judge, especially considering my own situation, but they were all little signs this family had been falling apart for a while.

"Want ice cream?" She asked, a wide grin appearing on her face as she held up the tub. "Chocolate chip."

I laughed for the first time all night, joining her at the bench. "Absolutely."

Passing me a bowl, she hesitated before asking, "Do you want to… talk about it?"

Instinctively, I shook my head, scooping the ice cream into my mouth. "Just wanna eat ice cream."

She smiled, but there was a certain sadness behind it that wasn't usually there.

I didn't want her to pity me.

No, I *needed* her not to.

She was the only person who had ever noticed something being off in my family, yet she had stuck by my side through it all. Never once did she treat me any differently because she believed I had it bad.

I couldn't have that change now.

Liv was the only constant in my life. A constant I wanted to keep.

"I'm not gonna ask you anything," Liv assured me, gently squeezing my hand. "But I need you to know that you can talk to me."

"I know that," I whispered, resting my head on her shoulder.

I did know that.

That was why she was the only person I'd never even considered running from.

I had Izzie and Josie, and I considered both of them good friends. The boys had always been wonderful to me as well, and I appreciated their kindness, but there was only one person who *never* made me doubt their loyalty.

That was Liv.

"Thank you," I whispered, and we both knew it had nothing to do with the ice cream or the sleepover.

Chapter five

February 17th 2004

SAVANNAH

I stepped through the gates of Ridgewood College, light brown hair tied into plaits with two navy bows, face carefully blank like I hadn't survived a war the night before.

Nobody would question it, though.

Because I'd been wearing long sleeves since the fourth grade.

By now? Everybody had just figured I got cold easily.

Except Liv.

I loved the rest of my friends to pieces, but I didn't open up.

Not anymore.

I'd become even more closed-off after the death of Marlee.

I caught a glimpse of myself in the window of the main building, the wideness of my grey eyes, the sleeves pulled low over my wrists, the carefully blank expression on my face.

My reflection looked just the way I intended: put together, untouchable.

The truth lived somewhere underneath all that.

"Hey, Sav!" Liv called out, cutting through the harsh breeze of the wind. Liv was sunshine in the human form. She bounced up to me, blonde curls everywhere, navy school jacket already slipping off one shoulder like it was allergic to staying put.

"Hey, yourself." My lips turned upward immediately.

Liv had that effect on everyone.

She found warmth in the darkest of people, and didn't even realise just how much of a strength that was.

She squinted at me, reading me in that way she sometimes did, like she knew I was half made of glass and half pretending to be steel.

But Liv was Liv. She didn't push.

Instead, her green eyes twinkled with joy as she slung an arm over my shoulder and steered me toward the courtyard where the rest of our friends were gathered.

"Sav." Theo winked as I slid into the seat beside him, usual mischief written all over his face. "Heard you and my buddy had a chat the other day."

Liv blinked at me, glossed lips parting slightly.

Yeah, I'd purposely left that detail out of each conversation with my friends this week.

I mean, it had been a small moment, right?

He'd stepped in to defend me when I was vulnerable, but anybody half decent would have done that.

I didn't figure anyone would see it as something more than it was.

It was silly of me to assume that, considering Theo and Archie had been attached at the hip since the beginning of time.

They were almost as close as Theo and Liv.

But nobody could beat them.

"Archie Bennett?" Izzie raised an eyebrow, the sharp tone in her voice cutting through the silence. "Really?"

"Casey and her bitchy friends were harassing the girl," Theo explained carefully, steering the assumptions away. "He stepped in to help."

Josie groaned, perched on the seat next to Izzie. "I hate them."

"Okay, change of subject," Theo declared, always the first to pick up on it when I was uncomfortable. "Livvy, pull your shirt down."

Liv looked down at her chest, the strap of her red bra slightly showing underneath her white shirt. "Struggling not to look, Theodore?"

"Struggling to keep my dick down, actually," he said casually, completely unaffected.

Izzie gagged. "Would you quit it?"

"What?" Theo raised a brow. "I'm majorly in love with her. I thought we got that."

"In love with her." Izzie rolled her midnight blue eyes. "More like you enjoy the thrill of the chase."

"Iz," Billy warned, handing her medication and a bottle of water. "Let's go."

She rolled her eyes, but complied anyway.

That boy was the only one she'd ever listened to.

After the night of Marlee's death, everything had collapsed in Izzie's world. She'd burned bridges with near everyone, and I assumed that's what put an end to whatever those two had going on.

Nobody could blame her for that, either.

She was *there*.

That night on the tracks.

She'd watched it happen.

Nobody else knew what truly went down on the night of her death.

Nobody but Izzie.

That was reason enough for people to put up with her anger and drastic mood swings.

Although, those had begun long before Marlee's suicide.

A few months after her death, Izzie had given us Marlee's suicide notes. She'd kept them for a while, unsure of whether or not she wanted us to see them.

A lot of our friends still resented her for that.

But none of us had even opened ours.

No one but *Izzie.*

I wasn't even sure Izzie's contained a proper explanation, because it was obvious she wasn't satisfied with whatever answers she had received.

"Callahan!" A familiar voice cut through my thoughts, and I blinked myself out of the haze.

There he was again.

For the first time all week, I was sitting in front of Archie Bennett.

He was here for Theo, of course, but I couldn't help the shiver that ran through my spine in his presence.

"Practice," Archie announced, but his beautiful eyes weren't on Theo.

They were only on *me.*

Why were they on me?

And why was I staring back?

"Savannah." He nodded in greeting. His tone was casual, but the softness behind his tough exterior told me something had shifted since that day. Instead of just seeing me, he was *acknowledging* me.

"Hi." I blinked, unable to tear my eyes away from his.

Liv nudged me with her elbow, her silent way of telling me I'd been staring for too long.

This was entirely unlike me.

I'd never had a boyfriend. Christ, I'd never had any interest in one.

So why the hell was my stomach doing flips?

"Look, I'd love to stay and watch the two of you do… Well, whatever this is. But we've got practice, Bennett."

"Right." Archie shook his head, tearing his eyes away from mine. "We have to go."

"So do we," Liv groaned, stepping up from the table, Josie doing the same. "We'll see ya later, Sav."

"Okay," I muttered beneath my breath, watching the four of them walk away, leaving me alone with my thoughts.

Liv and Josie cheered for the Ridgewood lions basketball team, leaving me alone for multiple hours each day.

Thankfully, Izzie didn't cheer. She was also the only one who had scored a similar score to me on last year's exams, landing both of us in Class A. I'd never been more grateful to have a smart friend.

Plus, it was a good thing I was the one to be put with Izzie.

The others got worked up too quickly, but I understood her enough to stay quiet while she worked through her whirlwind of emotions.

I may not have reacted in the same damaging way she did, but I knew that at the end of the day, we were both just teenage girls trying to get by.

I'd never blame her simply because her coping mechanisms didn't align with mine.

The bell rang, pulling me away from my thoughts once again.

Here goes nothing.

Chapter six

February 21st 2004

ARCHIE

It was finally the day of Theo's seventeenth birthday party.

Seventeen. The fucker was older than me, meaning he could have been graduating next year if he hadn't been so spectacularly dumb in primary school that they kept him back.

But no matter how much shit he received for that, I was secretly eternally grateful. Because if they hadn't kept him back in the third grade, I might have never met him. And as much as he killed me at times, I knew I wouldn't have made it through the past few years without the guy.

With pizza boxes and drinks littered across Theo's wooden coffee table, everything felt oddly perfect.

I hadn't felt this satisfied with life in a while.

Theo was sprawled out on the leather couch, one leg hanging off the side, making him look every bit the chaotic fucker he was.

Tonight, it was clear the repeat year had been worth it for him. Even though he had to live through another year of algebra which he described as 'personally insulting,' he got to be with the people who mattered.

"Theodore, could you please get me a drink?" Olivia asked sweetly, shooting him a wink, and I swear, I'd never seen a guy jump from the couch so quickly.

"Absolutely, babe. Vodka and coke?" He called from the kitchen, a mischievous edge to his tone that told me he already knew the answer.

"You know it," Olivia laughed, shaking her head.

My attention drifted away from those two idiots, and back to the rest of the party.

Olivia had planned a smaller party this year, considering the events of last year's one. Tonight, it was just our usual group and Theo's second circle of friends.

The girls.

Savannah.

Sitting right across from me.

Killing me.

Billy and Izzie were on the floor by the fireplace, Danny hovering near them like he had no intentions of letting them sneak off like he'd missed last year. As much as the two of them pretended to have moved on from the other, the unspoken language between the two of them was undeniable.

Theo re-entered the room with Olivia's drink a few moments later, stupid blue eyes shining as he sunk into the couch next to her.

A million stupid conversations later, Danny interjected, clapping his hands together. "Pack it in, the lot of ya. It's Theo's birthday, for Christ's sake. This only happens once a year," Danny chuckled. "Well, a year for those of us who understand the concept of time."

Theo leaned forward, catching onto the joke for the first time ever. "I repeat nothing." He pointed an accusing finger at Danny. "I didn't need that extra year. I was born a natural genius."

Danny snorted. "Is that what we're calling it now?"

"Hey!" Olivia shook her head, but there was a slight twitch in her lips. "Theodore is smart. He's just... well, Theodore."

Theo narrowed his eyes like he wasn't sure if that was supposed to be a compliment or insult.

"Yeah, you bloody bet I am. It's just fucking algebra. It's personally-"

"Insulting," Billy finished for him, head shaking in disbelief. "We know."

As the conversation spun into typical Theo territory; evil parrots and what not I, moved from my spot next to Danny and sat on the armrest next to Savannah.

"Hey there." I couldn't help the grin that appeared the moment her sweet, grey eyes locked on mine. "You look… lovely."

She did look bloody lovely. She wore a yellow dress that fit her body perfectly, and I almost couldn't tear my eyes away.

"Thanks." She smiled ever so slightly, but it was there. I felt my heart do an entire 360 spin, if that was possible.

Sure as hell felt like it.

My shoulder brushed against hers for a split-second, and I quickly leaned back into the couch like I hadn't even realised I was doing it.

Except I *did* know. And she *did* feel it.
Fuck.

I was already whipped, and I barely knew the girl.

I had never been interested in a conversation with a girl. Didn't care for it at all. But with her? I wanted her to keep speaking. I just wanted to hear her *voice.*

"You know, Olivia and Theo's thing has been there forever," I said, desperate to keep this conversation going with common ground. "I've seen it." I picked up my beer, swirling it slowly before pointing a finger at Sav. "You've seen it."

Sav blinked. "What?"

"I mean, Theo's always been the only one who knows how to get under her skin. And she lets him. Every. Single. Time." I shrugged. "Pretty bloody obvious, I reckon."

Savannah frowned, her gaze turning to Olivia and Theo. I followed her line of sight, and instantly noticed the way Olivia's attention was flicking between his eyes and his lips.

Yeah, there was something there.

Savannah blew out a shaky breath once she finally looked back at me. "I guess I noticed a little. Never thought too much of it, though."

I nodded, holding her gaze for a moment too long. Which, yeah, made me a total fucking hypocrite.

I couldn't dump shit on the two of them for pretending when I was sitting here doing the exact same thing.

I forced myself to look back at the others, not trusting what would happen if I kept staring into her grey eyes. All it would have taken was one moment, one second, and I would have given it all away.

Everybody was arguing now, teasingly ripping at each other's throats like they always did. But the truth was, they were all here for Theo. For our friend.

Half of us barely knew each other, but there was no question in showing up when it came to Theo. No hesitation.

Theo hooked his ipod to the speakers shortly later, putting on a playlist that couldn't have belonged to anybody but him.

For example, No Doubts' *'Just A Girl'* blaring from the speakers first.

Theo and Olivia headed to the front of the room, Josie following shortly behind, and singing every lyric with far too much enthusiasm.

In that moment, I wondered how anybody could get through life without friends like these.

Hell, half of them weren't even my friends, yet they still managed to cause a huge impact on my life each day.

We were all, without a doubt, forever intertwined.

Savannah laughed quietly, and even though small, it may have been the loveliest sound I'd ever heard. She didn't laugh much. It was a flicker of something precious before she caved in on herself again.

"I can't believe he will be eighteen next year," Sav said, actually *starting* a conversation with *me*.

She didn't do that often.

Christ, maybe this is why I attended parties.

"Not very good at adulting, huh?" I responded with a grin.

"Not at all." She giggled once more, her eyes flicking up to the front, everyone still performing. "Guess we'll just have to see where this goes, huh?" She added, so quiet that only I could hear, but I wasn't nearly dense enough to believe she was simply talking about the party. Or that's exactly what she was doing, and I was reading too much into this.

Regardless, I couldn't help the smile tugging at my lips as I spoke, "Guess we will."

Olivia accidentally knocked Theo off the couch then, pulling everyone's attention on them. That, or he'd said something idiotic and she'd done it on purpose. I never knew with them.

"Ah, babe. If I had a dollar for every time you purposely hurt me, I could actually afford to-"

"Alright. The only thing worth putting money on is the fact that you'll never make the right decision," Izzie fired with a grin, but there was a small bite to her tone.

"That's a low blow," Theo chuckled, sipping his beer.

"Not kidding." Izzie shook her head, still sat next to Billy by the fireplace. "You should at least take one thing in your life seriously." Her eyes deliberately flickered to Olivia, then back to him. "Before ya lose it."

Theo's grin faltered slightly, but he didn't let it last. "And because I don't sit around miserable all day, that means I don't take anything seriously?"

Izzie didn't flinch, didn't move. "No, because if you took one bloody thing seriously, you'd make even the smallest effort not to throw it all away. And I'm pretty sure that I could say one thing and your entire life would fall apart."

Theo took a step back. Not afraid, but cautious. "I'm not the enemy here. Let the anger go. Let. It. Go."

"Let it go?" Izzie cried out, voice raising to something dangerous. "Marlee is dead. Gone forever. And you act like it never happened."

"We are all grieving!" Theo snapped, not bothering to hide his anger anymore.

"Yeah? Well, not all of us could have prevented-"

"Iz." Billy shook his head, sliding his hand into hers. "We're not doing this tonight. Not to Theo."

That shut her up immediately.

Izzie's lips parted slightly, but quickly closed. She whispered something in Billy's ear then, causing him to nod and help her up.

"We're gonna get going," Billy said calmly, brown eyes flicking down to Izzie's wrist like he was searching for… something. Shit. "Happy birthday, Theo."

Then the door slammed shut.

"Well, shit," Theo chuckled, tone lighter now. "Hurricane Izzie."

The mood quickly shifted back to how it had been earlier, and it all felt easy again.

Thankfully.

Whether she could control her anger or not, I felt for Izzie. Truly. She was with Marlee that night. It must have fucking killed her to witness the death of her best friend, but I knew it was a grey area when it was one of them that she lashed out on.

It was rare, and I'm sure she believed there was reasons for that anger, but it happened.

I'd seen it happen.

And usually? It was either Liv or Theo that anger was misdirected to.

Savannah shifted uncomfortably on the couch again, clearly worried by the arguments.

Without thinking, I shifted closer and gave her a comforting smile. "You're all good, Savannah. It's all good."

That earned me another small smile from her, and I felt I was doing pretty good. I mean, I'd gotten smiles and a few conversations from the girl.

I was pretty sure that didn't happen often.

She didn't trust me yet, though.

Our conversations were short and simple, and I barely knew a thing about her.

But at least I'd been trying for some sort of friendship instead of going right in and kissing her like I wanted to.

That was a first.

I did wish she knew this wasn't normal for me either. Seriously, I'd barely spoken to any girls since I met her. I hadn't slept with a girl all month. While that's short for most people, I found sex to be some twisted type of coping mechanism. But it was almost like I met Savannah, and suddenly, my brain chemistry was rewired.

There was no reason for that. We were merely friends, let alone more. I didn't know why her existence erased any other girls from my mind, but it was happening.

Plus, my subconscious told me she was somebody worth keeping around.

Maybe, just maybe, there was something worth saving.

Fuck that, there was *definitely* something worth saving.

✦

I'm not sure how it happened, but everybody else had fallen asleep a half hour ago.

Everybody but me and Savannah.

We'd been sitting on the balcony since then, eyes fixed on the street lights bright and slightly blurred by the rain.

I didn't know what to say. I still wasn't quite sure how to speak to the girl.

But I couldn't *not*.

Not when this opportunity was standing *right* in front of me, practically begging me to take it.

I cleared my throat, the noise embarrassingly loud in the silence of the night.

Savannah didn't look at me. She kept her eyes ahead, protectively wrapping her arms around her small frame.

Does she not feel safe around me?

I shifted awkwardly, the metal chair creaking under me. Real smooth.

"You're extra quiet tonight," I whispered, looking at the stars above.

She took her time to reply. "Sorry. I was just thinking."

"You know what I think?" I offered, searching her eyes. "I think that you think too much."

She laughed, actually laughed, causing me to grin way too wide, way too fast.

"Maybe you don't think enough," she replied easily.

"I think." I nodded, leaning back in my chair. "But good to know I give off a thoughtless guy."

"No! I mean-" She ran a hand down her face, clearly embarrassed as she stuttered over her words. "That's not what I meant. I don't think you're thoughtless."

"What *do* you think?"

She thought for a moment before her lips parted slightly, just to close again.

She shrugged. "I don't know you well enough."

I hated that there was no yet at the end of that sentence.

But, truth was, I'd lost touch of who I really was after the death of my family.

I'd lost touch of *everything*.

"I… I should get going," she said suddenly, rising from the chair. "Thanks for sitting with me."

I nodded slowly. I wanted her to stay, I realised, but I had no choice but to watch her walk away. "I'll be seeing you."

Chapter seven

February 28th 2004

ARCHIE

After an irritatingly long fucking week, it was finally game day.

The one day each week that made the rest of this shit feel worth it.

The air was thick with the kind of electricity you only found when the whole school, the whole town, was watching. Ridgewood was undefeated this season, but it didn't matter. Today was different. Today, we were *facing* them. Ophelia Bulls.

What started the rivalry was unknown, but it was a real damn thing.

We had something to prove. *I* had something to prove.

They'd taken our spot in the championships last year, and we weren't about to let that happen again. I sure wasn't.

There was no backing down now. The boys had their game faces on already. Billy's jaw was clenched tight, Theo's eyes cold and sharp, and Danny? Even Danny, who didn't take this half as seriously as we did, was bouncing on his heels, trying to contain all the energy he always had but never knew how to use.

I couldn't blame them.

I felt the exact same.

This was the moment we'd been waiting for since the first day of school.

"Alright boys," Coach barked. "This one is important. Now, remember what I tell ya before every game. It's not about the win. It's about the fact that you *try.*"

"Alright, Coach," the team said in unison.

Olivia and Josie were already in the stands, voices loud as they cheered for us. Olivia's voice rang out, "Let's go, boys!" and Josie was right beside her, waving her pom-poms around, cheering loud enough for the whole school to hear.

But then there was Izzie. Her eyes were locked on Billy. For a second, I wondered what was truly going through her head. She usually struggled to contain her anger, but not now. Not with Billy on the court.

The two of them sure sucked at being exes.

And then… there she was. Savannah. Standing by the fence on the other side, her eyes locked on mine the second I walked onto the court. She offered me a small smile, and I matched hers with one of my own.

There was a tall guy on the opposing team that had 'Grey' etched into his jersey, so I assumed she was here for him.

Whoever he was.

Savannah had three younger boys attached to her hip, none of which looked like her. All of which looked like the other Grey.

Christ, that girls life was a whole fucking puzzle.

"Quit it," Theo muttered, nudging my shoulder. "You haven't taken your eyes off the bloody girl all day. Fuck that, you haven't taken your eyes off her all month."

I quickly teared my gaze away. "I'm not watching her," I mumbled, but I couldn't even convince myself.

He scoffed. "Whatever helps you sleep at night."

The whistle blew, sharp and demanding, pulling me back to what should have mattered most. The game had started.

The sound of the crowd was deafening, but all I could hear was the rush of my heartbeat in my ears, the pounding of my feet against the turf. I had to win this game. I *had* to. *Me*.

I'd been dragging this team along for years. I'd gotten us to multiple championships, and kept us afloat. There was no chance I'd let us fall now.

But as I glanced over at Savannah one more time, trying to convince myself that her stare wasn't something that made my chest tighten, there was something about the way she was watching me, that silent intensity... I couldn't shake it.

It was ridiculous.

Nothing had ever taken my attention away from the court. Not until now.

And I couldn't let that happen today.

Because today? It wasn't just a game. This was a war.

I grabbed the ball, dribbling around multiple guys and straight toward the hoop.

The only thing that mattered was the game, and right now, I was *all in*.

The opposing team surrounded me, and I made a clean pass to Theo.

Billy broke through the defensive line, his speed unreal, and the way Theo passed it to him felt almost instinctual. We'd all played together forever, and today, that connection was more valuable than ever. Billy faked left, stepped right, and for a split second, I could see the other team scrambling.

Coach pulled Billy off, replacing him with a fucker that had no hope. That meant this game was entirely on my back.

Five minutes later, the ball was back in play. We were winning 48-50, and I wasn't about to let that go down.

This was *our* game, and it couldn't slip away now.

The next few minutes felt like they lasted forever. Billy passed it to me. I saw an opening. I made the move.

7 seconds on the clock.

The ball was in my hands.

Score had went up to 52-52.

I couldn't have that.

I dribbled to the hoop, shoving the opposing team members out of the way as I got closer.

4 seconds.

I threw the ball.

2 seconds.

It bounced against the ring.

1 second.

Swish.

The crowd erupted into cheers, but my eyes… they weren't on anybody except the girl in the third row.

Savannah was looking directly at me now.

It wasn't even a question.

For a girl who barely showed emotions, the pride in her expression was painfully clear. Especially considering her brother's team had lost.

Yeah, I decided to go with brother.

But she was proud.

Was she proud of *me?*

Fuck, this girl was going to be the death of me.

"Bennett!" Coach called, grin wider than ever. "You did it, bud!"

A wide smile stretched across my face at his approval.

The cheerleaders were louder than usual.

The crowd was still cheering.

Coach had an arm hooked over my shoulder in an instant.

This was exactly what I lived for.

But fuck, I wanted my dad here to see it.

I pushed those thoughts down, unwilling to let them in when I'd won the most majorly anticipated game of the year.

I won it.

I did that.

I hated that I'd been staring at Savannah ever since the win. My eyes couldn't move away. They wanted to stay on *her*.

Both teams cleared out almost immediately, the crowd following shortly behind.

But not her.

Not Savannah.

She remained in the bleachers, shooting me a look.

One that said everything words didn't.

She felt it too.

Whatever the fuck this twisted emotion was.

Yeah, I had a feeling this would be a long ride.

I glanced around, double-checking that we were alone. We were. "Hey," I called out, heading toward her seat.

"Hey," she replied quietly, clearly uncertain. "I just… I wanted to congratulate you on the game. You played really well."

"Huh," I breathed, eyes widening slightly at her openness. "Thanks, Savannah."

"Yeah." She nodded, pausing for a moment. "I'm not too sure why I stayed."

I tilted my head to the side. "Do you need a lift home?" I offered, dangling my keys. "Everyone else is gone."

She hesitated, biting down on her lip before nodding. "If you don't mind?"

"Course I don't."

We didn't speak for the first few minutes. The car was quiet, aside from the low hum of the radio, a song neither of us really knew playing softly through the speakers.

Savannah sat with her knees pulled to her chest, arms wrapped around her body as she stared into the night like it held all the answers.

I tapped the wheel with my thumb, subtly glancing over. "You always this quiet, or is it just me?"

She cracked a tiny smile, barely there. "Depends on the day."

"Right. Well, let me know if I ever make the list," I said lightly, turning onto a much busier road.

That earned me a small laugh. "You might already be on it."

"Yeah?" I asked, sounding almost too curious.

She smiled, but didn't let it show for long. "We'll see."

I smiled too, even if she couldn't see it.

"You were good out there," she told me again, voice softer now. Less worried. "Like, really good."

I shrugged, trying not to let her praise get to me. "Thanks."

"Yeah." She nodded slowly. "You look like you belong when you're out there."

I glanced at her, but she wasn't looking at me anymore. I couldn't tell if she meant that as a compliment or something else entirely.

"Do you?" I asked before I could stop myself. "Feel like you belong anywhere?"

Her silence stretched just a little too long.

"Sometimes," she finally said, shrugging.

That stung more than I expected it to.

Because fuck, I cared, and I hated the idea of her feeling alone.

Because she wasn't.

I was right here.

Savannah didn't see that yet.

She would. I'd make sure of it.

We pulled into her street, the glow of the streetlights casting long shadows over the dashboard. I slowed to a stop outside her place, leaving the engine running.

She didn't move to get out. Not right away.

She was always hesitant.

"Thanks for the ride," she murmured.

"Anytime," I said. And I meant it.

✦

An hour after driving through what might have been the roughest part of town, I pushed the front door open to find an empty house.

It was a good thing, considering my brown hair was still dripping with sweat from our win and every muscle in my body ached in the best way.

Christ, I needed a shower.

The adrenaline was still coursing through my veins, but the loneliness overtook any sense of joy I'd been feeling.

The silence.

It never got easier.

I inhaled a shaky breath, flopping onto the worn-out couch as I tried to escape the demons in my mind.

It never worked.

The car crash.

As it did every time the house was quiet, my mind instantly drifted back to the worst night of my life.

It always felt like the kind of thing I should have been able to push away when needed, but it gnawed at the edges of my mind every damn day.

Every time I closed my eyes, it was all I could see. The shattered glass, the fire, the twisted metal.

My baby sister Elsie with a sad smile on her face like she knew exactly what was about to happen, and had come to peace with it.

She was thirteen. Fucking thirteen years old when she died that night.

She still had so much ahead of her.

I hated myself for being unable to prevent it. I was in that car. I was the reason they even got in the car in the first place, damn it!

The rain was heavy, and we all knew it was dangerous. So bloody dangerous. But I just couldn't give up my last fucking game of the season.

The guilt of that never quite faded.

Because if I had been man enough to sacrifice one single game, I could have stopped it. I *would* have stopped it. They would still be here.

But I didn't. Now Elsie was gone. And so was my dad.

Beforehand, it had been a wonderful night. Elsie was giggling the whole time, making strange jokes and bringing warmth into the world like she always did.

It was perfect.

Until it wasn't.

Dad swerved the car off the road to avoid colliding with another, and I screamed, not even realising I'd been doing it until the world turned upside down. The screech of the tires, the cries from Elsie's mouth. It was all too loud. Too *much.*

I couldn't breathe. I couldn't move. And when I looked to my right, Elsie's head had slammed against the window, green eyes wide open but completely lifeless.

Dad was already out cold by the time I forced my eyes open, head slammed against the steering wheel.

I couldn't save them. For a while, I wasn't even sure I'd be able to save myself. Maybe that would have been easier. That way, I wouldn't be living in a world that stopped making sense the moment their hearts stopped beating.

The ringing in my ears was unbearably loud, and my entire body was aching and unable to move.

The next thing I knew, I'd somehow managed to escape the car, stumbling across the road to get help but nobody was there. I was on my own.

Then I saw her again. Elsie, still in her seat, but her body crumpled and lifeless.

The blood…

The glass…

The fear…

I couldn't save her. I couldn't save my dad.

Eventually, after crawling through the blood of my lifeless family and searching through the pocket of my dad's denim shorts that were ripped to shreds, I found a phone. I called for help.

I got out.

I survived.

But it didn't matter. Because nobody could save them. They were already too far gone.

The guilt never went away. The guilt of being the only one to make it out. The guilt of surviving when *they* didn't.

I should never have survived it. Not if they weren't allowed to.

Theo had shown up at my house that night once the paramedics gave me the okay to go home, and he just sat there and held me for hours while I cried.

I'd never cried in front of anybody until then.

But I didn't care.

For that whole year, he was all I had. Danny and Billy truly did make an effort to show up, but Izzie was completely fucked back then too.

She needed somebody, and I couldn't blame them for that.

I couldn't do anything but sit by and watch as my entire world collapsed. Mum was utterly depressed, never leaving her bed, and letting the guilt and grief take over until I could barely recognise her.

Theo proved his friendship that night. He didn't care that I cried. In fact, I could tell he was holding back tears of his own. They'd become his own family, after all.

He opened a bottle of whiskey he'd stolen from his step dad's cabinet, and poured us glasses.

He didn't force me to talk about it. He didn't ask any questions once I'd gone silent. He just assured me anything I felt was normal, and told me I had his unconditional support no matter what.

At the time, he hadn't really known how to deal with it. After all, you can't understand the weight of parental grief until you've experienced it. But it was only a few months later that his mum was hit by a bus, and the roles were reversed.

It was a fucking train-wreck of a year.

There had been so much loss I could barely breathe when I thought about it.

But, at the end of the day, Theo was there. I always knew he was a fucking great friend to have in my corner, but when things fell apart back then and I needed him more than ever, he hadn't hesitated once. He discarded his usual mask of humour and showed up. Stayed.

Even after his own mum's death, I never once doubted that he would show up the moment I needed it.

Sometimes, I wished he would admit that he needed it too.

For so long, we were all the other had.

That was enough.

He also had Olivia, though.

Because even though their situation was complicated and downright confusing, they never ran from it. They knew the love was there.

Me? I was a coward.

Basketball. Parties. A few friends. Random hookups every now and then.

That was the plan.

Was I allowed to want *more?*

Chapter eight

March 5th 2004

SAVANNAH

I wasn't ready.

Not really.

But Marlee's letter was staring back at me from beneath my pillow like it had been for the past eleven months, and I knew I'd left it unread for too long.

Her name was below mine in her favourite blue ink, slightly smudged like she knew she was running out of time.

If not for me, I had to do it for *her*.

For the girl she was.

For her memory.

Marlee wrote those letters in hopes that somebody would read it. She wrote them so somebody would *finally* know her truth.

She didn't write them for no reason. She knew what her plan was. She knew that night was going to be her last.

But she still spent it writing these letters.

That meant she *needed* someone to *know.*

But I wasn't ready to lose her.

Not then. Not now.

This letter felt like losing her all over again,

But for the first time since April last year, I slid the envelope into my hands.

I pressed it to my heart.

One second.

One moment.

And then, with trembling hands, I opened it.

Hey, little bestie.

It is with a heavy heart that I write this letter, knowing I will never be able to say these words to your face. I know I'm a coward for taking the easy way out, and no words will ever be able to explain my great despair to leave you like this.

You were one of my favourite people in the world, Savannah Grey, and I need you to know that there is absolutely nothing you could have done to change my mind.

Please, please don't blame yourself. You were never a reason to leave, but one of my few reasons to stay. I'm sorry there weren't enough to keep me around.

I have kept so much from you and everybody else, and I can't apologise enough for keeping you in the dark.

I know I'll never get the chance to make this one up to you, but I need you to know that wherever I am, I'm happier. I wish we had more time together, but please know that I loved you like a sister and there is not a bone in my body that ever doubted your eternal kindness and compassion. The love and support you showed me over the years will never be forgotten.

I didn't want to do this. I fought for so long to prevent this being the end, and I need you to know that I tried.

You are, without doubt, the strongest person I ever met, and I didn't want to put another weight on your shoulders.

I didn't deserve to confide in you after my lack of belief in your father's abuse caused you so much pain.

Somehow, you trusted me enough to be the one person you could confide in that day, and I brushed it off. That day plays on an endless loop in my mind, and I cannot even begin to tell you how sorry I am.

I love you, Savannah. And now, it's my turn to confide in you. I can't go without you knowing the truth...

I slammed the envelope closed with a swift move of my hand.

I couldn't keep reading.

It was selfish. I knew that.

Marlee deserved her truth to be known. But I wasn't somebody strong enough to do that for her.

Maybe the girl I used to be could have found the courage, but she was long gone.

I couldn't know what pushed her over the edge that night.

Worst of all… I couldn't stop blaming myself. What if I'd noticed sooner? What if she'd told me? What if I'd been the one with her that night? What if I'd known?

God, if only I'd known.

But I knew, deep down, that no matter how many times I asked myself these questions, the answers would never change.

Because Marlee was gone.

Forever.

And I should have saved her.

I was *supposed* to be the savior.

Chapter nine
March 8th 2004

SAVANNAH

It was thirty-three degrees. Normal for Australia, yet it still killed me every time. I'd lived in the small town of Ridgewood my entire life, but I never got used to the heatwaves.

My patience was fading faster than the small amount of mascara I'd put on, a useless attempt at hiding the sadness and vulnerability in my eyes.

Liv was late. Again. And the longer I stood there baking in the school carpark with two bags and a short fuse, the more I wondered if this friendship came with workers' compensation.

That's when I saw it. The black Toyota.
Same model. Same stupid, blaring radio.

Without thinking, I yanked open the passenger door and climbed in, dumping both bags on my lap.

"Finally," I muttered beneath my breath, not even looking over. "You said ten minutes, not twenty."

Silence.

Then, a voice that was absolutely *not* Liv's.

"Well, this is quite unexpected."

I froze.

"We meet again."

I turned my head slowly. Carefully.

There he was.

Archie Bennett.

I shouldn't have kept noticing.

But God, he was gorgeous.

His eyes were locked on mine, brown hair slightly damp from training, with muscles that had no business looking that good in uniform.

I squinted, hoping that would change the image. It didn't.

"Not that I'm complaining," he chuckled, dark green eyes piercing my soul. "Just didn't see ya as the carjacking type."

"I-" My voice caught in my throat. "I don't… I mean- oh my god. I forgot you had the same car. I thought you were-"

"Liv," he finished, smirking.

"This isn't… God, I'm sorry."

"You didn't think to check the driver?" He raised a brow, clearly amused by my humiliation.

"I didn't look!" I hissed, grabbing my bag off my lap and practically kicking the door open. "I am *so* sorry."

But before I could escape to someplace safer, easier to understand, his deep voice followed me out.

"You know, I could still drive you."

I turned. "What?"

He shrugged casually. "Already made yourself at home. May as well finish the ride."

"It's fine." I shook my head, still mortified. "Liv will be here soon."

"Pretty sure she left with Theo."

Hell.

My cheeks blazed with heat, lips parting.

But behind the mortification, something flickered.

Archie Bennett offering *me* a lift?

Again?

We barely spoke. Before that day in the hall, Archie and I had only ever exchanged polite nods.

My first and only car ride with Archie hadn't been nearly as bad as I anticipated. In fact, I enjoyed it. But I was out of line here. I could feel myself wanting to let him in, and that wasn't a part of the plan.

"Come on. I don't bite." He grinned. "Not unless you're into that."

"Please stop talking," I sighed, sliding back into the car. "Are you sure? It's out of your way."

"Huh. You're a polite carjacker." He brushed a strand of dark brown hair from his forehead, starting the engine back up. "Don't ya worry. I have to go in that direction anyway."

I didn't want to come across as curious. Truly, I couldn't have cared less. But the only places around my area were dodgy houses, graveyards and liquor stores. He was too young to go to the liquor store. Well, he was also only sixteen and too young to be driving alone, but I chose to ignore that fact.

Liv was younger, after all.

Nobody around here really listened to the law.

The questions came before I could stop myself. "First of all, how do you remember where I live? Second of all, where could you be going around Chappell street?"

A flash of something less cocky appeared on his face, but disappeared just as quickly. "I remember because it wasn't all that long ago I drove you home. And… I'm going to the graveyard."

My head snapped up. "The graveyard?"

"My dad and sister," he explained like it was easy, but I could see the grief in his eyes. It was all too familiar. "They died in a car crash a few years back."

A hint of sympathy rushed through my veins. "Why are you telling me this?"

"I'm not secretive." He said, pulling onto the road. "Plus, you seem like the type that can keep a secret."

Oh, if only he knew…

"Of course." I nodded in reassurance, feeling the desperate need to comfort him. "Um… I'm sorry that happened."

"Ah, don't be," he brushed it off, but his hand visibly tightened on the steering wheel. "Can I ask you a question?"

"Can I stop you?" I forced out, willing myself to keep it together.

'What was she like?" He asked gruffly.

Was.

It'd almost been a year, but the use of past tense still cut through me like a dagger.

"I'm sorry," he said, clearly noticing the way my entire body tensed at the mention of Marlee. "I just… she used to say hi to me in the hallways even though I barely knew her. She was lovely."

"Marlee said hi to everyone." A sad, brief smile appeared on my face.

"Yeah, that's why everybody misses her." He shrugged slightly. "Sorry, by the way. About her."

I swallowed. Didn't look at him. "Thanks."

He kept mentioning her.

I didn't understand.

Everyone else either zipped their mouths and erased her name from their vocabulary, or they spoke of her like she was gossip.

I appreciated the way he asked about her, though. He didn't see her the way did. Even though he wasn't close with Marlee, he was one of the only people who acknowledged she meant something.

Maybe he genuinely wanted to know about her.

She was a spectacular person, and my life would have been bland if Marlee McGovern had never appeared in it.

But it would certainly be happier if she hadn't been erased from it.

"Do you like music?" He changed the subject by asking, giving me space.

"Everyone likes music."

"Fair enough." A small chuckle escaped his lips as he turned on the radio.

'Fade into you' by Mazzy Star was the first song to play.

One of my favorite songs ever written.

He hummed along to the lyrics slowly. I couldn't bring myself to meet his eyes.

I knew I shouldn't have been thinking about him. Not for any reason.

But God, it was almost as if he haunted me.

He wasn't an easy one to forget.'

But those thoughts quickly disappeared, because I felt it as soon as the car slowed.

Home.

My body tensed, and I could only hope he missed it.

"This you?" He asked, pulling into the familiar cracked driveway.

I nodded, immediately reaching for the door handle. "Hey, uh… thanks for not making that any weirder than it already was."

He huffed a laugh. "All good."

I laughed for the first time all day. Slightly.

I stepped out, slinging my bag over my shoulder.

"I'll be seeing you," Archie called, shooting me a wink.

I nodded slowly.

Yeah, I had a big feeling he would be.

I rushed for the door, feeling his lingering gaze on my back. I needed him to stop looking at me, because against all of my rules and morals, I wasn't sure that I was capable of looking away first.

Chapter ten

March 17th 2004

ARCHIE

The lights were blinding, casting shadows across the entirety of Josie Whitmore's house. People were everywhere. Clustered in corners, hidden in bedrooms, taking shots in the kitchen, their voices almost inaudible beneath the music.

Parties were nothing new.

This was routine.

Parties. Girls. Numb. Repeat.

But tonight cracked the pattern.

Because *she* was here.

And that changed *everything*.

I couldn't pretend it was a surprise. She was the reason I'd made an appearance tonight. Simple as that. I told myself it wasn't about that. That I just needed the noise and the alcohol to drown out everything else. But that was a lie, and I knew it.

Moving through the crowd and ignoring the shrill laughter of drunk girls sliding their hands up my arm, I glanced over to the back.

There she was.

Savannah.

Her voice was quiet, especially against the chaos of the night, but I was instantly drawn to her.

Truth is, I'd been drawn to her that very first day. Not gradually, not gently.

I had no choice in the matter anymore.

The girl did something to me that I'd never felt before, and I wanted to rip it out. Or hold onto it forever.

Her eyes darted around the room as she laughed with Olivia, and each time somebody walked through the doors, a smile tugged on her full lips,

Fake. I could see that.

I took a swig from my bottle, not bothering to check which drink it was. It didn't matter.

The look in her lonesome grey eyes caused an ache to bloom in my chest, and I felt like I'd been fucking shot.

Her eyes were heavy with something.

Something guarded.

Something *broken.*

Christ, I just wanted to know the girl.

But it felt like she was always running away. Not physically, maybe, but Savannah Grey was *always* halfway out the door.

Without thinking, I pushed through the crowd, making my way towards her.

But just as I broke through the crowd, another girl stepped in front, blocking my way.

Pretty. Lipglossed. Familiar?

"Archie." She tilted her head, eyes glossy and knowing as her hand brushed my cheek. "Wanna get out of here?"

I hesitated.

Last month, I would have said yes without thinking. Hell, I probably already had. She looked the part.

Plus, I'd probably been with the girl already.

But I couldn't… I couldn't.

Because Savannah was watching me from across the room.

Her expression was unreadable, but I could've sworn there was a new flicker of sadness behind that exterior of hers.

Maybe not.

But she hadn't even started letting me in.

And if I walked away, I'd be slamming the door before it even had a chance to open.

For the first time in a while, I didn't want the easy option.

I just wanted *her.*

"No," I replied quietly, removing her hand as it slid to my arm.

"No?" She repeated slowly, frowning. "You *never* say no."

"Sorry," I muttered, clearing my throat as I sidestepped her.

Yeah, that was probably a dick move.

But I couldn't find it in me to care right now.

Running a hand through my hair, I managed to slide through another group of girls, reaching the drinks table.

When she saw me, her eyes flickered for a second before she looked away, like she was trying not to make it obvious she noticed me.

"Hey," I said, the word coming out a little rougher than I intended.

She didn't meet my gaze, just gave me a slight nod. "Hi."

"You good?" I asked, even though I knew the answer.

She stiffened, her fingers tightening around the edge of her cup. I could see her pulse flicker at the side of her neck, like she was calculating something in her head. A second passed before she looked at me.

"I'm not exactly a party person," she admitted quietly. "That's all."

My stomach twisted at that, but I couldn't put a finger on why.

"Do you wanna go somewhere quieter?" I heard myself ask. "I mean, it's loud in here, and you seem uncomfortable…"

She hesitated, her gaze darting around the room like she was trying to find an escape.

"I'll be fine." She nodded, offering me a small smile. "I'm staying here tonight, so I'll just go up to one of the rooms," she said, sidestepping me.

Yeah, apparently, I wasn't allowing that.

"At least let me take you upstairs," I offered, searching her eyes. "There's a lot of people around." A lot of guys I don't trust.

She sighed, but the resigned look in her expression told me she agreed. "Yeah, okay then."

We both headed in the direction of the stairs then, our silence becoming less awkward as the music grew louder.

I stood close enough to make sure nobody else could reach her, but still kept a respectful distance between us.

The stairs creaked beneath our feet as we made our way up, but the noise faded quieter the higher we got, and her body turned visibly relieved the moment we were out of easy view.

"Which room?" I asked, glancing around. The hall was dimly lit, the yellow lights calm in contrast to the flashing ones downstairs.

Savannah paused, her hand lingering on the doorframe of one of the rooms. Her eyes flickered from the handle to the floor, looking at anything other than *me*. I wasn't enough of a dick to think that was coincidental.

"Um…" She started, trailing off. "Thank you."

Savannah blew out a shaky breath, nudging the door open with the tips of her small fingers.

But the room wasn't quiet.

No, there was…

What the fuck?

I turned, rushing back into the room she'd entered.

Izzie Harris was in the corner, sobbing into her hands, glasses smashed all over the room.

"Izzie," I heard Savannah whisper soothingly, running a hand through her friend's dark blonde hair. "Hey, can you hear me?"

"Do you need help?" I heard myself ask, immediately alarmed.

What the fuck is going on?

"It's fine." Savannah waved me away, an unfamiliar defensiveness to her tone.

"You're sure?" I continued, unwilling to leave this situation unattended.

I knew Savannah could handle… whatever this was.

But that was Danny's sister in there.

I couldn't exactly leave her like that. That'd break a million of those stupid fucking codes he was always rambling about.

Savannah sighed, gesturing for me to step outside with her.

"I can handle it," she whispered once the door was closed, determination clear in her voice. "It's not... unusual."

"This has happened before?" I asked, vaguely gesturing to the door.

"She has bipolar." Savannah raised an eyebrow, covering her mouth with her hand as she saw the way my expression changed. She thought I *knew*.

Bipolar?

How the fuck had Danny never mentioned that?

Shit. That explained... everything.

"Bipolar?" I repeated, frowning. "Why didn't Danny tell me that?"

Savannah thought for a moment before her grey eyes widened slightly. "She might not have told him?" It sounded like more of a question than an answer.

Not told him?

Her brother?

"How the fuck would Danny not know his sister has bipolar?" I asked, thoroughly shocked.

Savannah shrugged helplessly. "Maybe she wanted it to stay secret."

Was she asking me to keep a secret?

From Danny?

Well, shit.

"Please," Savannah pleaded, voice barely above a whisper. "It's not my secret to tell. It's not yours, either. I figured she'd told him, but…"

"Are you asking me not to tell Danny?" I squinted.

"I don't know." She ran a hand down her small face, clearly confused. "I just… you know as well as I do how easily things fall apart in her world. If you tell Danny, that will *break* her. Especially if she never got the chance to tell him herself."

"How is that fair on him?"

"Time hasn't passed for her," Savannah explained carefully, more open than usual. "For the rest of us, it's almost been a year since Marlee died. But for her? That was only yesterday."

Realisation dawned on me. "She's still living that night."

Savannah nodded. "She's living in *hell*."

"And if I told Danny…" I trailed off, thinking to myself. "If I mentioned the bipolar to Danny, I'd be the one to send her back?"

Savannah bit down nervously on her lip. "I don't think it would be fair to blame that on you entirely, but… maybe. Look, I won't tell you to keep this secret. But I just needed you to know what could happen if Danny knew," she continued. "She clearly hasn't told him for a reason."

I nodded stiffly. "Look, if she's not in danger, or dangerous…"

"It's under control," Savannah confirmed.

"Then I see no reason to speak about it." I offered her a smile of reassurance, glad to see her opening up even if it was a bit forced. "You're *very* perceptive, by the way."

"Thank you… Archie." She tilted her head, grey eyes clear of that usual guardedness. "You're uh… you're nice."

I chuckled. "That much of a surprise?"

Instead of her usual, anxious reaction, she matched my laugh with one of her own. "You know that's not what I meant."

Yeah, I knew that.

After a few moments of silently looking into my eyes, Savannah gave me a slight nod. "I should go back to Izzie now."

I smiled in understanding. "I'll be seeing you."

Savannah sighed. "I'm pretty sure you will," she muttered beneath her breath, clearly meant for herself.

But I heard it.

I heard *her.*

I saw *her.*

Yeah, this was getting real bad, real fast.

Chapter eleven

March 25th 2004

ARCHIE

I *had* been asleep.

For some reason, Olivia had called me at three in the morning, demanding I get to her house ASAP.

I was sure it couldn't be important as her words had been followed by laughter, but Olivia was Theo's sidekick.

I wasn't about to ignore the girl.

Drawing in a ragged breath, I reached my hand up, but the door flung open before I had a chance to knock.

Olivia stood in front of me barefoot, wearing a hoodie that I suspected belonged to Theo, holding a damn bowl of popcorn at 3am on a weekday.

"Took you long enough," she scoffed, stepping aside to invite me in.

I yawned. "Yeah, well you called me in the middle of the night."

"No, I called you at the start of the morning," she corrected with a smirk.

"Alright, well, is your house on fire?" I asked, my eyes darting around.

"With excitement." She wiggled her eyebrows.

I tilted my head in confusion, stepping inside.

Christ, everyone was here.

Danny and Billy were stretched across the couch, Theo playing with a lighter he shouldn't have had, Izzie and Josie half asleep on one of the beanbags.

"Bennetts here," Olivia announced like I was royalty. "We can finally start."

"Start what?" I asked, struggling to keep my eyes open.

Theo chuckled from the floor, a mischievous glint in his eyes like he knew something I didn't. "Savannah's birthday."

"Oh?" Yeah, that pulled me out of my sleep haze. "And when is that?"

"The 30th," Josie explained, suddenly wide awake. "But we wanna go to the beach on Saturday."

"Tomorrow?" I lifted a brow.

"Yeah, for those of us who slept." Danny groaned, resting his head on the back of the grey couch. "The girls wanted us all to spend the night at the beach. Apparently, that takes seven people to plan."

"Hey!" Josie threw a handful of popcorn at him. "You were excited earlier."

Danny rolled his eyes. "Sorry, Jose."

"So," I started, still confused. "Why couldn't you tell me this over the phone?"

"This is much more fun, don't you think?" Olivia said sweetly, throwing a piece of popcorn in the air to catch it in her mouth.

"You're becoming a pro, babe." Theo shot her a wink.

"You know it."

Half exhausted and half confused, I decided to join them on the couch.

"You in?" Theo asked then, leaning in with that eager grin of his.

I didn't even hesitate. "Of course I'm in."

"You barely even know her." Izzie's eyes narrowed, clearly in one of her bitter moods. "Why are you here?"

I stayed silent.

It was hard to argue with the girl after seeing her in that state at Josie's party.

Christ, the bipolar explained everything.

"Does Savannah know?" I asked, desperate to change the subject.

"Nah, she'd back out," Olivia said. "I told her she could stay here tomorrow."

Theo gave me a look then, one that told me he knew exactly why I agreed to go. "We figured you'd be the one to make sure she actually comes."

"Yeah?" I asked, trying not to sound too eager. "She might not want to."

"She will come, because she won't *know*," Olivia said simply.

I nodded.

"Okay, Theo, bring your shitty speaker," Danny chuckled, shoving a handful of popcorn into his mouth.

"I resent that," Theo muttered, seemingly offended.

The group fell into full party-planning mode then, but I just layed back against the couch.

Christ.

Savannah's birthday.

I didn't even know.

But how was I going to survive a whole night on the beach with her? Yeah, I hadn't figured that out yet.

I let my mind drift off to Savannah.

Just this once.

The way her smiles never stayed. The way she always looked like she was ready to bolt.

Yeah, I'd find a way to save her.

Even if it killed me.

Mia Jade

Chapter twelve

March 26th 2004

SAVANNAH

I actually went along with it.

Olivia had managed to trick me into a camping trip for my sixteenth, and I hadn't fought it.

I'd just… let her.

The thing is, Olivia didn't even have to beg. She just looked at me with those puppy-dog green eyes like I deserved something more than broken glass and slammed doors, and I agreed before I could stop myself.

That scared me a little. Because if I started wanting more... what happened when I couldn't have it?

Wanting was dangerous.

I'd learned at a very early age that I wasn't somebody who could wish for more. For better.

Because it never happened.

I could have become a christian and prayed to God everyday that my father would get better. That my mother would look at our family and realise how much pain she caused by staying.

But now? I knew that would never change.

Wanting only ever left you with disappointment.

I couldn't let those thoughts linger, though. Because I was surrounded by people who had shown me the *true* meaning of love.

We'd just arrived at Jolene beach after a two and a half hour drive, and it was much quieter than usual.

All I could hear was the waves hitting the shore and the occasional rustle of the trees. It almost felt too peaceful considering the usual chaos of my life, but I was enjoying it.

Golden hour had painted the beach wonderfully, and for a moment, I let myself believe. In happiness. In safety. Because hope was all I could cling to.

Izzie and Billy had arrived hours before us, and I could already see them unpacking everybody's tents.

Both of them were looking at each other like they had something to say, but nobody was actually speaking.

She kept looking at Billy like she wasn't sure if she wanted to kiss him or slap him across the face, and I had absolutely no idea what was going on with them. Though, it had always been like this. Flames and silence.

When we were little, they were practically inseparable. Liv and I used to joke that if those two didn't end up together, love wasn't real.

But now that things had fallen apart, it felt like watching two people orbit the same planet but never quite *land*.

"Savannah," A familiar voice called, dragging me away from my thoughts. "Happy early birthday."

I turned to see Archie with that usual boyish grin on his face, wearing his usual laid back confidence that would work on any other girl.

Something felt different about him today, though. A little too careful, even. It felt like he was trying not to look at me for too long. Or maybe I was just imagining it.

My heart thudded like it didn't trust me to stay calm. Stay *normal*.

"Archie?" I tilted my head, approaching him carefully. "You came?"

He nodded, slightly lifting an eyebrow. "You seem very surprised."

"Little bit," I admitted with a nervous laugh.

"Well, don't be." He grinned, grabbing the eski from the boot. "Like it or not, I've come to think of you as a friend."

A friend.

I could do that.

"Right," I agreed, grabbing the rest of the drinks from the car.

"Where's everybody else?" Archie asked then.

"They're all setting up over there." I gestured to the bottom of the empty beach, the sunset sending shadows across the sand.

"Are you okay?" He caught me off guard by asking.

"Of course I'm okay."

"Okay, you just… you don't look happy," he said quietly, shaking his head. "You never look happy."

God.

"I'm- I am happy," I said, hoping it was enough to convince him.

Even though it didn't entirely convince me.

But I was okay.

I thought so, anyway.

Thankfully steering away from those conversations that were not going to be had, he gave me that smile. The one that always seemed to break through my walls. The one that made me feel like he could already read me too easily.

I turned away before I could feel that ridiculous flutter in my chest again.

From day one, I knew this boy was a bad idea.

But when he looked at me like no one ever had, like he believed I was worth sticking around for, it was hard to remember.

"Sav, are we sharing a tent?" Liv called from the group.

She and Theo were already unrolling the blankets and laughing, clearly in their own little world already. I tried not to think about how much that bugged me.

Not the fact that they were happy, of course.

Because I knew there were a lot of things unspoken between the two of them, but I couldn't help the ping of jealousy I felt, knowing that some people allowed themselves to love.

But I'd never say that out loud.

"Yeah," I replied with a smile, raising a hand to my forehead to block out the sun. "If you're sure?"

She shot me a wink before grabbing our tent from the pile. "Of course! I get the birthday girl."

Everybody started to pitch in then, causing a quick flurry of movement along the sand. Danny and Josie were now arguing over where the firepit should go, and Izzie still kept glancing at Billy like she was waiting for him to say something. He never did.

"Hey, wanna set up over here?" Archie was beside me again, and before I had the chance to ask what he meant, he was already spreading a blanket along the rocks where we could see the ocean, but it made it feel more private. Intimate. I wasn't sure if I liked that.

No, I did.

But I shouldn't have.

"The views nice, huh?" He said, half to himself as he stared up at the sky.

Bad idea, Sav, I reminded myself. *Sit with somebody else.*

Instead, I sat down. With him.

Of course I did.

"You okay?" His voice was softer than usual, like he was genuinely worried about me.

I almost wished he didn't care.

That would've made it a whole lot easier.

Because if I believed he didn't care, I'd already be gone. I wouldn't have to question the way my chest ached when he smiled, like he was something I knew I'd never quite have.

If he didn't care, I wouldn't keep finding myself memorising the lines near his eyes when he laughed or the way his voice dipped when he needed to be serious.

He made me believe I wasn't as broken as I'd always thought. And that? That was scary.

Because when people see the good in you, they expect you to live up to it.

And what if I couldn't?

What if he got closer and managed to see the mess I was hiding?

I nodded quickly. "Of course. Just... birthdays."

Did I just half open up to him?

Uh oh.

"I get it." His voice was so quiet, so gentle, that I almost couldn't hear it over the wind. "But you're here now. That's what matters."

"Shouldn't you be... I dunno, out, charming someone else?" I asked, fiddling with my fingers, never meeting his gaze.

"Nope." He offered me a genuine smile, leaning back to watch the sunset. "I'm good right here."

Was that flirting?

Was he flirting with me?

No.

I leaned back too, keeping a decent amount of space between our bodies.

But our knees were resting achingly close, and I realised something.

Archie Bennett, against all of my wishes, had become one of the first people I wanted to keep around.

That wasn't to say I hadn't been contemplating running off, because that's exactly what I was doing.

But he just… I don't know. In some twisted way, I suppose he brought me hope.

And while hope was something to cling to, I'd come to learn it was the most dangerous emotion of all.

We fell into silence then. It wasn't awkward anymore. It was somewhat comfortable.

"I've got to grab more firewood," Archie suddenly said, standing up and brushing the sand from his jean shorts. "You coming with?"

My eyes darted around.

Being alone with him was almost certainly a bad idea, but everyone else was already in their own worlds, and it seemed I had no control over myself when this boy was near.

I trailed after him, away from the group and to the forest area besides the beach. The stars had appeared now, the orange glow from earlier now a sky of darkness.

"So, your actual birthdays in a couple days," Archie said, and it wasn't a question. He *knew.*

I nodded, wrapping my arms around myself to warm up as the ocean breeze filled the air.

"How does it feel?" He asked, reaching for wood.

I let out a small laugh. "Just another year, isn't it?"

"I guess." His voice was quiet as he shrugged. "But it's *your* day. Another year for *you*. You deserve to feel..." He trailed off like he was unsure of what to say, but I felt it all the same. More.

I stopped in my tracks, turning to face him for the first time in a while. He was standing a little too close, his face almost too perfect under the flashlight. I swallowed hard, willing myself to act casual.

I wasn't sure why, considering there were no words coming out.

So I just looked at him.

Yeah, weird move, Savannah.

I blinked hard, tearing my eyes away from his. "No, I know that. I mean… I just don't find them important."

He nodded, eyes flicking down to my shivering arms. "You cold?" He asked.

"No, I'm okay," I attempted to protest, but he was already pulling his grey hoodie over his head.

"You take it," he insisted, holding it out. "I've got another, anyway."

Pressing my teeth into my lip, I pulled the hoodie over my head.

I almost laughed at the size of this hoodie on me. I wasn't short exactly, but Archie was practically a giant.

"Thanks," I whispered.

"Anytime." His entire face softened, and it felt like we were the only two people in the world. "You know that."

Yeah, I was starting to get his drift.

But I needed him to *leave*.

Because I couldn't bring myself to walk away from the boy.

He paused, reaching into his pockets like he was searching for something. "Wait a sec. I, uh… I got you something."

I blinked, confused. "What?"

"For your birthday," he said casually, a small chain tangled slightly around his fingers. A silver necklace with a tiny charm. An infinity sign, I realised, delicate and shining.

My heart skipped a beat, lips parting slightly.

I didn't speak.

What the hell was I supposed to say?

"It's stupid," he said quickly, clearly regretting it already. "I'm just… it's your birthday. You don't have to wear it or anything." He scratched his jaw.

I took it from his outstretched hand, brushing his fingers with mine.

"It's not stupid," I said quietly.

He nodded, exhaling a breath of relief. "Can I?" he asked, gesturing to my neck, and when I didn't stop him, he stepped forward gently, carefully, brushing my hair aside and clasping it behind my neck.

I couldn't breathe.

His hands were too close to my body.

Yet, somehow, never close enough.

"There," he said, barely above a whisper. "Looks good on you."

He stepped back, and I could feel the charm resting just below my collarbone. It felt heavier than it looked. Or maybe it was just everything it meant.

"Happy early birthday, Savannah."

I swallowed, offering a smile before falling back into step with him.

The woods were darker a few minutes later, the stars barely bright enough to cut through the branches overhead.

Neither of us had spoken in a while, but I could feel him walking beside me.

My hands were shaking slightly, and I told myself it was because I was still cold.

But I knew it wasn't.

I knew it was him, and the strange effect he had on me.

He made me feel safe.

And safety was something I'd learned to fear. Something I'd stopped trusting a very long time ago.

I turned my gaze back to the ground, my heart beating so loud it was the only thing I could hear. I couldn't help pretending this moment, the necklace meant nothing at all. I also couldn't ignore how much it *did* mean. But I wasn't ready to say it.

There was too much baggage involved.

✦

The vodka was definitely working.

Danny, usually quite rational and calm, had just face planted into the sand after convincing himself he could do a cartwheel. Twice.

I was safe and happy.

It felt almost... fake.

"Okay!" Liv shouted, clearly not realizing the loudness of her tone. "Truth or dare, birthday edition! Sav, you're up first."

"No," I groaned, but I was laughing along with everybody else. "Okay, okay. I pick dare."

Izzie, who was being unusually lovely, let out a dramatic gasp. "Oh, she's brave. The youth."

"Iz, you're younger than her," Billy reminded, pulling her closer to his chest where

Izzie had taken up permanent residency about an hour ago.

Usually, I would be questioning this behaviour from Billy, but the alcohol was clearly working wonders.

Theo grinned. "I dare you to skinny dip."

Liv's head shot up. "You said that awfully quick."

"Theo. Shut the fuck up." Danny nearly choked on his drink.

"Yeah, well. I should have expected to get in trouble," he sighed.

"I am not skinny dipping," I said flatly. "I may be very drunk, but I'd like to keep my dignity for a while longer."

"I would," Izzy added dreamily. "But I sort of can't feel my legs."

Everybody burst out laughing, and just like that, we were little kids again.

Archie still wasn't speaking much. He was next to me, arm lazily draped over the seat, but he was entirely absent.

Theo randomly chuckled to himself then.

Like, non stop, head-thrown-back laughter.

The group fell into the sort of chaos you can only experience with people you entirely trust, and it was lovely.

Liv was singing the lyrics of *I Want It That Way* by Backstreet Boys, using a stick like it was a microphone.

Billy and Danny had formed a very intense alliance against the laws of physics, arguing about whether fire would burn faster in space.

I hadn't laughed like this in forever.

For one moment, just one, I felt like I belonged. Like this strange group of people was exactly where I was supposed to end up.

I caught Archie watching me then, not saying anything, just smiling softly like he could see that something had shifted in my mind.

I didn't smile back.

Not because I didn't want to.

But because I didn't want to *want* to.

Theo's laughter loudened, stealing everyone's attention.

"You gonna share it with us?" Danny raised an eyebrow, chugging another beer.

"I was just thinking about when I came here with Livvy and Sav a couple years back."

My mouth opened at the memory. "Was that when you stole that goat?"

"He stole a goat?" Archie asked, suddenly vocal as he glared at Theo. "Why the fuck did you steal a goat?"

"The story makes it sound bad," Theo explained between chuckles. "He was all alone."

"On a farm!" Liv cut in. "Where goats are supposed to stay."

"Yeah, well I didn't *know* that," Theo defended.

"Nobody raised him," Izzie stated like it was no big deal. "Can't judge him for not knowing farm animals."

"Iz." Billy shot her a WTF look.

Izzie's eyes widened in realisation. "That's not what I-"

Jesus.

Yeah, everyone hurried off to their tents after that.

Everyone except me and Archie.

"Sav?" Liv called, poking her head out from our little blue tent. "Are you coming to bed?"

I glanced at Archie beside me, the only person left before giving Liv my attention. "I might stay out here for a bit. If that's okay?"

She grinned, eyes darting between Archie and I. "Sure."

Then she was back in the tent, and we were alone.

Alone.

That was dangerous.

Why I did that? Unsure.

But God, I wanted to be able to let this boy in.

"You okay?" Archie asked, voice low. "It's been a long night."

I nodded, suddenly hyper-aware of how close he was. "Yeah, I'm good. It's been... nice."

I felt his fingers brush mine. Barely. Like he wasn't sure if it was on purpose or not. My hands tensed slightly, but I didn't move away.

"I should go to bed," I heard myself say before standing up, the moment shattering like glass.

"Savannah," he said abruptly, causing me to turn.

"Yeah?"

"I like your eyes," he slurred, heading for his tent. "Even if they're keeping secrets from me."

Chapter thirteen
March 30th 2004

SAVANNAH

Me and the girls were curled up in Liv's
bedroom like we had been a hundred times
before, the fairy lights above her bed bringing a
certain warmth to the room.

It was my sixteenth.

Like every year, it felt more like a funeral
than a celebration.

Liv, as sunshiney as ever, had made vanilla
cupcakes. Josie bought some cheap beer she
swore her mum wouldn't miss. Izzie didn't bring
anything, but I think that was the point. She was
never the one to say happy birthday or shower
me with presents, but she was always the first to
sit close and make sure nothing slipped through
the cracks.

Liv passed me a cupcake then, her smile almost *too* bright. "Go on," She said, her smile fading slightly. "You're allowed to wish."

"Just another year to survive," I murmured, no longer feeling the need to lie around these girls.

Maybe they didn't know just how deeply rooted my trauma was, but they'd been there for a lot of it.

Our Birthdays were very few nights of the year where we weren't pretending.

Because we all wanted Marlee to be here, even if none of us were brave enough to say it.

"You survived fifteen," Josie said softly, reaching for another cupcake. "That's something, isn't it?"

Marlee never made it to fifteen.

God, she was haunting me more than usual tonight.

Instead of voicing that, I nodded and slid the cupcake into my hand.

"I miss her," Izzie said suddenly, her voice flat but not cold. That was a *good* sign.

She didn't look at any of us, but we all looked at her.

"We all do." Liv offered a smile, but this one barely reached her eyes.

"I thought it'd get easier," I heard myself admit. "But the older we get… the more I realise she won't, you know?"

Won't laugh. Won't cry.

Won't fall in love or mess up or heal.

Izzie reached over and rested her head on my shoulder, a quiet weight that said more than any words could.

Izzie didn't let herself be soft.

That's why, the moment she did, it meant more than any words possibly could.

"I know," she whispered.

"Let's make a toast," Josie said after a few moments of silence, lifting her cheap beer. "To Savannah surviving fifteen."

"To making it through sixteen," Liv added, her voice soft but sure.

Izzie didn't say anything, but she raised her bottle.

I looked at my cupcake, one bite taken, then set it down and lifted my drink.

"To the girls who stayed," I said, voice steadier than I felt. "And the one who didn't."

We clinked bottles gently.

No one said cheers.

No one needed to.

"I have something that will cheer you guys up." Izzie gave us a rare grin, turning her back to face us before lifting her pink tank slightly.

"A tattoo?" Liv gasped, reaching out to trace the small, blue infinity tattoo on Izzie's lower back. "When did you get this?"

"Last Thursday," Izzie admitted proudly.

"Were you having a…" Josie trailed off, but we all knew what she meant.

And we all knew the answer.

"Of course I was." Izzie frowned, turning to face us again. "But I don't regret it." She shrugged, sliding her shirt down to cover it. "So, do we like it?"

"I like it." I took a small bite of the vanilla cupcake. "I think it's nice. You're very brave."

"You're scared of needles?" Izzie asked, but she wasn't mocking me. She was sincere.

"Little bit," I said quietly.

No, I just don't trust men with needles near my body.

"Are you gonna tell us about it?" Josie pried then, tilting her head back to look at me.

"About what?" I asked, cheeks slightly flushed.

"Archie," Liv giggled, taking yet another huge bite of her cupcake. "You've been around him a lot."

I rolled my eyes, dismissing her assumptions. "I barely know him."

"But you want to." Izzie squinted, pointing a finger at me. "You want to, don't you?"

I considered lying, but I just shrugged helplessly instead. "Maybe?"

Liv offered a smile before saying, "I think he's worth getting to know."

Josie frowned, deep in thought. "I agree."

"Might be something worth saving," Izzie agreed.

Izzie's agreement meant something more than anything else could.

Because Izzie Harris didn't agree with anything unless she wholeheartedly believe it.

Was he somebody worth sticking around for?

It was hard to tell.

But what I did know is that this boy was making it utterly impossible to run from him.

It wasn't like I'd tried.

I wanted to be around him.

All the time.

He had a way of calming my life. It was almost like no matter the violence, the chaos and the sadness of my life, his presence alone was enough to make me forget.

Even if for only a moment.

◆

1.5 seconds.

That was how long it took between me entering the house and my father knocking me to the floor.

Jayden texted me an hour ago, telling me dad was on the warpath and staying out was a bad idea.

My phone hit the ground first. Then my shoulder. Then my pride.

I didn't cry. Didn't flinch.

That part of me had learned how to go still.

He stood over me, breathing like a bull, and said something slurred and spit-soaked that I didn't even try to make sense of. I just stayed quiet. Let it roll past.

I never understood how I'd been born into such a family.

While my brothers were all good people and in no way comparable to our father, their first reflex was anger. Mine had never been.

Each one of my brothers also looked like our parents. I never understood how I'd missed out on those genes, but I was eternally grateful to lessen the connections.

When he finally stumbled off down the hall ten minutes later, muttering curses at ghosts, I stayed on the floor a little longer than I needed to.

The tile was cold under my cheek. My ribs ached in a familiar, dull way.

Eventually I pushed myself up, heading straight for my bedroom.

Jayden peeked in a few minutes later, his face pale and tight. "You okay?"

"Fine," I whispered.

He didn't believe me. But he nodded and went back to his room anyway, because what else was there to do?

We knew there was no chance of getting out.

And I also knew that there was no chance of us all making it out *alive*.

I quickly reached for my door handle, turning it back and forth until it locked. Not that it would change anything.

Our father was strong. Clearly, stronger than us.

Breaking down doors, for him, was an easy task.

But I liked the comfort of knowing there was that extra protection anyway.

That's why Jayden had saved up money from work last year, so he could sleep without worrying as much.

I leaned against my door, my head pressed to the wood.

There were things I could have done tonight.

Or a million nights ago.

Called somebody.

Ran.

Screamed.

But we had tried it all before.

And now, we'd just had to accept the fact that maybe this would be our reality forever.

Chapter fourteen
April 7th 2004

SAVANNAH

The stadium was buzzing with the sort of excitement that only existed on nights like these.

That was the weekly basketball game.

For whatever reason, tonight was more important than usual.

Other than Ophelia Bulls, Jayden's team, they also had a rival team from outside of town. The eagles? I don't know.

Regardless, Danny had insisted I attend the game with Izzie.

I could spend the game pretending I showed up because I'd been asked to, or I could admit the truth.

The fact that I only came for Archie.

The boys ran onto the court then, causing a chorus of cheers from the ridiculously massive crowd.

Izzie flinched.

Barely. But I saw it.

She had her hoodie on even though it was boiling, arms folded tight around her chest like armour. It was small, but I could see her legs trembling even though she tried to stop it.

"Want to leave?" I offered, nudging her knee gently with mine. "I'm happy to go."

She glanced at me, and the sharpness in her expression faded almost instantly. "No, I've got you," she said, pausing for a second. "I've got you, right?"

I tilted my head, a small smile playing on my lips. "You've *always* got me."

She smiled, her silent way of saying *thank you, please don't leave me.*

I had no plans of ever doing so.

I stuck by Izzie for so long because I believed she was good underneath it all. She spent her whole life wrestling her own mind, and I hated when people assumed she was cruel for that.

But that's because I knew this version of Izzie.

The girl who always tried impossibly hard to be good, to stay kind, even when it broke her beyond fixing.

Though, I didn't believe that.

I thought she'd be just fine one day.

The whistles blew, signaling the start of the game, and the cheerleaders were so loud I could barely hear myself think.

Liv and Josie were in the front, looking just as perfect as ever.

Liv's blonde curls were in a neat braid, courtesy of her mother being a hairdresser, her green eyes filled with excitement and determination. Josie had the very same look on her face, auburn hair falling into her face.

I loved watching them cheer.

They just looked… at home.

So much so, I'd almost been convinced when they begged me to join the team.

I had the skills. I knew that, because I'd done cheer a few years ago.

But I felt that rejoining now would be like regaining control over my life, and that would be a faux.

I didn't have that.

Not at all.

Archie grabbed ahold of the ball, my eyes tracing him like the back of my hand.

He looked wonderful on the court.

Well, the boy looked great anywhere, but on the court… It looked natural. Like this was his habitat.

He dribbled down from the other end of the court, effortlessly shooting it straight through the hoop.

I didn't think he had a single doubt, either.

He *knew* he was good.

A few months ago, I would have seen it as cocky or arrogant. But now? I'd be shocked if he didn't brag about those skills.

He was seriously impressive.

His dark green eyes met mine then, sending a shiver down my spine.

He held my gaze for a second too long. That second was enough. Enough for me to know I was well and truly *screwed.*

Coach Holloway blew the whistle then, pulling the boys into a huddle. Most people knew him as the boys' basketball coach, but he'd also taken over the cheer team last year when the school couldn't find anyone else. A strange combo, but somehow, it worked.

Ridgewood was ahead 42-45.

2 minutes.

The boys' were back on a split-second later, all of them using every muscle in their body to assure they stayed ahead.

I knew they would.

I had no doubt.

Because they had Archie Bennett for a captain.

And I'd come to know him. I'd come to realise he wasn't just some stuck up basketball guy, but one with a heart.

One with a heart that I wanted to know better.

But I couldn't.

Ugh.

Just *ugh*.

One hoop after the other, and Ridgewood had the win.

You know, I never really understood basketball. But Archie's eyes went straight to mine once those whistles blew, and I was suddenly very grateful for James Naismith.

Suddenly, my feet were moving without permission, and I was in the middle of the court, surrounded by basketballers and the girls who cheered for them.

And I was moving toward Archie.

Walk away, Savannah, I told myself. *Turn around.*

Of course, I did the exact opposite.

My heart wasn't listening to the more sensible parts of my body.

"Sav!" Archie called from the other end of the court, ball still in hand. "You came."

"Theo asked," I brushed it off by saying, even though we both knew it was bigger than that.

A few more steps, and I was standing directly in front of the boy I'd spent months wishing not to like.

But I did.

Yeah, really bad.

"So... you won," I said, awkwardly fiddling with my hands. "Um, good job."

"Thanks." He grinned, his head turning to where Coach Holloway approached us.

Instead of stopping in front of Archie, he stopped in front of *me*. "Savannah Grey." He tilted his head, offering me a smile in greeting.

"Hey Coach," I responded, looking to Archie for answers.

He just shrugged.

"We have an empty spot on the cheer squad," Coach informed me. "And... it's yours if you'd like it."

Mine?

A spot on the cheer squad?

Christ.

I swallowed hard. "You want me on the squad?"

Coach nodded proudly, not a hint of uncertainty in his expression. "Take a few days to think. But it's a great opportunity, and I think you could be a wonderful addition."

"I'll do it," I blurted out.

What?

Did I just say that?

Coach raised an eyebrow, his wrinkles becoming more obvious, clearly just as surprised as me. "You will?"

No! "Yep."

"Alright, kiddo." He smirked, holding his thumbs up before backing away to the locker room, leaving me alone with Archie. Once again.

Archie cocked a brow, but I could see the pride in his expression. "Cheer, huh?"

"Cheer." I nodded slowly, confused by my own actions.

My eyes darted around the gym then, finding that everyone had cleared out.

Including my friends.

Yeah, I figured that wasn't an accident, but an opportunity to force me into time with Archie. Not that I was complaining.

Archie pulled keys from his pocket, swinging them around his finger once before glancing down at me. "Do you need a ride?"

"Yeah," I said softly, eyes locked on his. "Thanks."

The walk to his car was quiet, not the awkward kind, but the one that only appears between two people who have the weight of a million unspoken words hanging between them, begging to be addressed.

"You okay?" he asked, voice low but clear.

Rubbing my temple, I shrugged. "Are we pretending that didn't just happen?"

"You joining the cheer squad?" he asked. "No, I think we're very much not pretending."

I sighed, slipping into his car. "I don't know what I was thinking. I wanted to say no."

He snorted. "But ya didn't. Plus, I think you'll be good."

"You do?" I asked, voice coming out with a desperate need. A need to hear *his* opinion.

"Yeah, Sav." He shot me a wink, turning on the engine. "I think you'll do wonderful."

My heart did that thing again. The one that made me believe it wasn't mine anymore.

A few minutes into the drive, he shifted in his seat. "You don't have to prove anything by joining cheer, you know that?"

"I know," I muttered, pressing my teeth into my bottom lip.

He nodded, and thankfully, didn't push further.

Before we could pull onto my road, his eyes darted down to my slightly shaky hands. "Do you wanna... not go home?"

My head snapped up. "What?"

"I know a place," he offered gently before murmuring, "Plus, I wouldn't mind spending time with you." It was barely audible, but it happened. And God, so did my heart tripping over itself.

"Okay," I heard myself say quickly. Too quickly.

I fiddled with the seatbelt like it was some kind of rhythm, distracting my nervous mind like always, and it felt like nothing had changed.

Except everything had.

Because somewhere along the line, I'd grown quite fond of the boy in the driver's seat.

We drove for a while.

Maybe a few minutes.

Maybe an hour.

He drove around these wild twists, only breaking a few times to allow the kangaroos across the road.

He pulled the car to a stop, headlights shining over the rocky edge of a cliff.

I could see our town just below, flashing lights and every little building.

Wow.

He did know a place.

The world from here… it didn't look so scary.

It looked possible. Hopeful.

I slowly opened the door, heading to the edge. I glanced down, watching over our town, hands tucked into the pockets of my grey hoodie Archie let me borrow on my birthday, like maybe this was all a dream I'd wake up from soon.

Sure, it was a pretty dream, but it wasn't one that could last.

Because he gave me hope.

I wasn't sure I could handle any more hope being ripped straight from my hands.

When I was around Archie... I felt like I could tell him things. Things I'd never voiced aloud before. I felt like I could open myself up.

"When did you start coming here?" I asked, smiling. The first one all night. "It's lovely."

He joined me at the edge, sitting close, yet not close enough. "Before my dad and sister died."

I swallowed hard. "Right." And before I could stop myself, "Guess we both have a thing for the past."

Archie chuckled slightly. "I suppose."

I nodded, fiddling with my infinity necklace before glancing up at him. "Why are you nice to me?"

His head snapped up, genuine confusion written all over his face. "What do you mean?"

"I mean, you don't have a reason to be."

"I have a lot of reasons," he whispered, offering me a genuine smile. "A lot."

I tilted my head, willing myself not to break infront of this boy. "Thank you."

"Don't thank me." He shook his head, waving a dismissive hand. He paused for a moment, rubbing his jaw thoughtfully. "Can I ask you a question?"

"Okay."

"Do you know… do you know why she did it?" He asked, a thoughtful look in his eyes. "I know she had mental health issues, but did anything else happen?"

Marlee.

We were back on that.

Oh god.

I knew I needed to talk about her eventually, but when I tried, it hurt so bad I could barely breathe.

Her image flashed in my face, brown curls framing her pale face so perfectly, and those gorgeous green eyes, so bright they could light up a whole city.

"I don't know the full story," I heard myself admit, finally bringing myself to speak on her name. Honour my friend. My girl. "She'd been bullied, but that… that can't have been all."

"You think there was more to it?" He asked, frowning slightly.

I shrugged, because what else could I do? "I wish I knew."

As if he picked up on my utter devastation when I spoke about her, he allowed us to fall into silence.

"Hey, Sav?" He whispered a few moments later, gazing into my eyes with sincerity.

"Hi, Archie," I responded, cheeks slightly flushed.

"Don't run away."

I swallowed, my eyes fixed on the ground.

I won't, I mentally told him. *No matter how much I want to.*

Chapter fifteen

April 14th 2004

ARCHIE

Savannah Grey would not stay the fuck out of my mind.

Since that night on the clifftop, something had shifted. For better or worse.

She had opened up. Maybe not much, but for her? That meant a whole lot.

And I saw it. The way her eyes softened for just a second too long. The way her hands shook when she talked about things she usually buried. When she talked about Marlee.

She let me see behind the mask. Not all the way, but enough to ruin me over and over again.

I should've felt relief. Or hope. Or something remotely human.

But all I felt was guilt. Sharp, acidic, choking.

Because just as I started to understand Savannah Grey…

The less I thought about my dad and Elsie.

And that wasn't because I forgot them, or the grief shrunk. Christ, that wasn't the case at all.

But keeping them out of my mind, even for one second, felt like betrayal.

But thinking about them felt like drowning.

I was damned if I did and damned if I didn't.

I didn't have a *dad.* I'm not sure if I'd ever realised the eternal sadness that loss dumped on my life until this very moment, but, fuck,, it was killing me.

And Elsie. Her face never left my mind. Her laughter was forever ringing in my ears.

When I let these thoughts in, I was transported back to that night again.

And that night... Christ, that night almost killed me.

Literally *and* figuratively.

I truly didn't believe I'd make it out of that car alive. And the worst part? I didn't *want* to. Because no matter how much I thought that I believed there was a chance for them that night, I knew Elsie and dad were too far gone to be saved.

I just wanted to hold onto hope that if I found a phone, if I called somebody... I could fix it all.

Put the pieces back together.

But at the end of the day, I was only a thirteen year old boy.

"Archer!" My mothers' voice broke through my thoughts, pulling me back into the present with a loud knock. "There's... well, there's a girl here to see you."

A girl?

What the fuck?

I thought I'd made my feelings pretty bloody clear. Apparently not.

I groaned. "Yeah, just tell her-"

Then the door swung open.

I was sure my eyes weren't working right.

I tried squinting, but the image remained the same.

Yeah, that was Savannah Grey.

In my *house?*

"You're in my house," I stated, raising an eyebrow.

"Archer, that's not a very nice welcome to give the girl." Mum shook her head, gesturing for Sav to join me.

She took a careful step in, a weak smile plastered on her face.

Shit... it was almost April 20th.

Mum closed the door gently behind Sav, leaving us privacy.

"Are you okay?" I sat up, instantly alarmed.

"I'm- I mean, I'm sorry for coming here, I just needed-" She tripped over her words, frowning.

"Hey, hey. Sit down," I soothed, scooting closer but making sure I kept a respectful distance between our bodies. "Talk to me. Or don't. Whatever works."

She looked up at me, grey eyes sadder than usual. "Marlee. They want me to speak at the one year memorial and I..."

Fuck.

"You don't have to do it if you don't want to," I said, my hand moving to gently squeeze her shoulder without thinking.

She flinched.

Flinched.

Because of *me*.

"I'm sorry." I shook my head, quickly removing my hand. "I didnt even-"

Cutting me off, she slid her small hand into mine. "I want to do the speech. But I'm... I don't know, I'm scared."

I stopped breathing for a second.

Because Savannah Grey didn't *do* scared.

Not out loud.

And now she was sitting on my bed with puffy eyes and a voice that cracked, and all I wanted to do was wrap her up in something safe.

In my arms.

Where I could protect her forever.

Yeah, this girl had me completely.

"It doesn't need to be perfect," I told her. "You don't need to do it perfectly. Not for them. And definitely not for Marlee."

"I don't want to mess it up," she admitted quietly, subconsciously squeezing onto my hand tighter. I let her. "There were a million things I should have said. Now I have the chance, and I just…" She trailed off, letting out a breath that sounded genuinely painful. "I need to get it right this time."

"Do you think that if you'd noticed the signs, she wouldn't have killed herself?" I asked, thoroughly searching her eyes. "Because that is certainly not the case."

"I… I don't know. Maybe?" She said honestly, giving a small shrug.

Shit.

Yeah, I'd been there.

Am I supposed to tell her that?

"You couldn't have changed the outcome." I shook my head firmly. "I think you were one of the very few people in Marlee's life that made it bearable. Just because the bad outweighed the good for her, that doesn't mean it meant nothing."

She offered a weak smile, a tear trickling down her cheek.

God, I just wanted to hold her. To protect her from this.

I sighed. "You'll keep blaming yourself."

She looked up at me, eyes widening a little bit. "What?"

"It'll take a while until you see that it wasn't your fault, even though you probably know that somewhere deep down. But it will happen. It will always hurt to think about her, but one day, you'll be able to do it without completely breaking down. One day, you'll be able to remember the good parts even though it ended badly. and, Savannah? If I know one thing, it's that Marlee didn't want you to be sad. She wanted you to live your life to the fullest, even if she wasn't there to see it."

By the time I stopped the words from flowing, there were tears streaming down her cheeks.

Yeah, my arms involuntarily moved then.

One moment I was holding onto her hand, and the next, my arms were wrapped around her small frame, holding her impossibly close.

And I would have kept her like that forever if it was possible.

"You're gonna be okay," I whispered against her hair. "You're gonna be just fine."

She sniffled then, not bothering to hide her sadness behind that usual tough exterior of hers.

And still… I could only wonder if she'd be back to unreadable tomorrow.

God, I hoped not.

A few minutes later, she released her tight hold on me.

And that's when I saw it.

The ugly, purple bruise on her shoulder. A bruise that didn't belong on her pale skin.

My breath caught, my chest tightening with a mixture of anger and dread.

"What happened here?" I asked, eyes fixed on the mark.

She adjusted her hoodie, pulling it back over her shoulder far too quickly. "I fell down the stairs yesterday."

"The girls at school?" I frowned, trying to keep the anger out of my voice. "Did they do something?"

Her eyes flicked up, fast. But then she gave this tiny shake of her head, barely visible. "No. Our stairs aren't steady."

I wanted to push harder. To demand the truth.

But there was something in the way she looked at me then. Not scared. Just tired. So, so tired.

And for once, I let it go.

Maybe I shouldn't have. Maybe I should've thought deeper into it.

But in that moment, she needed something else.

"I believe you," I heard myself say. "But if anything ever is wrong, I need you to tell me."

She glanced at me, eyes more trusting than usual. "I promise."

Thankful, I nodded stiffly.

"Hey, Archie?" She continued, voice soft. Sad. "Will you be at the memorial on Tuesday?"

Without hesitation, I said, "Of course I will."

"Okay," she whispered, suddenly rising from my bed."I should get home now."

"Yeah," I agreed, showing her to the door. "I'll be seeing you."

She smiled. It was small, but it was definitely there. "You will."

With that, she was gone.

Chapter sixteen

April 20th 2004

SAVANNAH

This week had been nothing short of a disaster.

Dad was angrier, Marlee had officially been gone for a year, and I let Archie in.

I let him in.

It was stupid, really, but he was one of the first people to be nice when I was sad.

There was no turning back now.

I blinked myself back into the present moment, that familiar ache returning.

The chapel smelt like roses, but no amount of flowers could cover up the pain that filled this room. Everything felt still. Too still. Like the world had stopped spinning just long enough to let us honour Marlee.

I sat near the front, hands clenched tightly in my lap, the folded letter digging into my palm.

My fingers were numb, but I couldn't let it go. Couldn't let *her* go.

I felt weird.

Being here, preparing to read a letter in front of hundreds of people when I hadn't even been brave enough to read her last words felt selfish in a way.

Like I didn't deserve to honor her when I hadn't even heard her full story. Her full truth.

Someone sniffled behind me. Another one sobbed. But I couldn't look up. Couldn't move.

I had thrown up three times this morning just thinking about today, and now my heart was thudding against my ribs like it was begging to claw its way out.

After Lila McGovern spoke, they called my name.

I didn't move at first.

My legs weren't under my control.

But then I stood, legs shaking just enough to remind me I was still human, still alive, even when she wasn't.

The room blurred slowly as I made my way to the podium, gently unfolding the piece of paper like if I made a single crimp, I'd be tearing her away from me all over again.

God, grief was weird. Taunting.

Looking out at this crowd, this group of people who all came together for one reason… It was bittersweet.

I blew out a shaky breath, tipping the microphone just low enough for me to reach.

Archie's green eyes found mine from the middle row, giving me a small nod of encouragement.

That was enough. For me, that was enough.

I cleared my throat. "I… Um… I'm going to say a few words about Marlee. Well, to Marlee."

My voice sounded small. Croaky. Wrong.

"I don't know if I'll get through it, but…" I met Archie's eyes again, bringing me some twisted sense of hope in this storm. "But I'm gonna try. For Marlee."

I looked down at the paper. My hands were shaking now, but I kept going.

"Dear Marlee. Even now, I keep waiting for you to walk through the door. Sometimes, it feels like a cruel dream. Like maybe I'll wake up and you'll just… be there. I thought if I wrote this down, maybe it'd make more sense. Maybe the words would line up and explain what doesn't feel real. But nothing can quite fill the hole that you left in my heart. Our hearts," I started, voice cracking slightly. "You were complicated, but you were good. You were scared, but you never stopped being soft. Kind.

And when you cared about someone, which you did most people, it was fierce. I don't know much. But I know this: We don't blame you. I loved you, Marlee. I still do. And I always will. Wherever you are, I hope you're happier than ever. I hope it's quieter. And I hope you know we would have done anything to keep you here."

The words came to an end.

The crowd applauded, a mixture of claps and sobs filling the silence.

The priest offered a small nod, taking my spot on the podium. "Let's take a moment to remember a girl who was very dear to each and every one of us. Marlee McGovern."

I drew in a long breath, slowly returning back to my seat as the crowd grew silent.

I saw Izzie first. She was glaring at Liv's adopted brother, Adam, who sat in the back row. There was something angry in her look. Like he didn't *deserve* to be here.

I wasn't in a mood to observe, though.

I was just... tired.

I squeezed my eyes closed, the noise of the announcements fading into the background.

"Savvy!" Jayden called, clearly desperate.
I forced my eyes open, still half asleep.
Looking up at the clock on the wall, I saw that it was barely three in the morning.

Had the boys been hurt?

I rushed to my bedroom door, immediately inviting Jayden in. His eyes were red and puffy, body almost... limp.

"What happened?" I asked, scanning his body, but there were no bruises. "Did dad wake up?"

He shook his head, still silent.

"What happened, Jay?" I demanded, panicking now. "Please tell me."

"You should... um, you should sit back down," he said softly, sitting on the edge of the bed.

"No!" I argued. "Are one of the boys hurt? Jayden, I need you to-"

"Marlee's dead."

The words landed like a gunshot.

I couldn't breathe?

Marlee?

My Marlee?

No, no, no. This was all wrong.

For a moment, I thought I'd misheard him. "What?" I whispered, voice barely audible. "Say... say that again."

Jayden's face was hollow, entirely drained of colour. I could only imagine mine looked similar. "Marlee's dead, Savvy. I... fuck, she killed herself." He ran a hand down his face, and I could have sworn there were tears.

Jayden didn't cry.

He didn't cry in front of me.

He didn't cry in front of anyone.

This wasn't a joke.

"Jayden," I choked out, tears falling freely now. "Stop it. That's not funny."

"I'm not joking." He shook his head. "That wouldn't be fucking funny, Savvy."

"No," I shouted, pacing my room. "No, no, no. Jayden. How?"

He rubbed his temple. "I don't fucking know. Danny Harris called."

"Danny?" I asked, none of this making sense. "What if he's wrong. How could Danny possibly-"

"Izzie was there," he said, voice drained of personality. "She was with Marlee."

There was no way this was real.

But it was.

It was. It was. It was!

I broke into sobs then, collapsing in my brother's arms. "H-how? Jayden, I should have known," I choked out, sniffling against his shoulder. "How did I not see it? How could this have happened?"

"I don't know, Savvy," Jayden said softly. "I'm so fucking sorry."

I couldn't hear him. I closed my eyes, my body trembling.

I wanted to scream. To break something. I wanted to run to Marlee's house and hold her in my arms so she could never leave me.

But it was too late.

It. Was. Too. Late.

✦

"You did really, really good, Sav," Archie told me in the graveyard, all of us laying flowers down on Marlee's grave.

"Thanks," I whispered numbly, taking a seat beside him on the grass. "It definitely didn't feel like it."

"It doesn't," he agreed with a small shake of his head. "But you did wonderful. Everyone was proud. I was… I *am* proud of you."

I felt my expression soften then, finding comfort in his presence. "Thank you."

Being around him made me forget it was still a dangerous idea.

But I missed my friend, and I didn't want to go home, and God, everything was just *wrong*.

Would it be so wrong to want happiness for myself?

To have something that was just for *me*?

It felt like too much of a risk.

But if I'd realised anything over the past few months, it was that this situation was out of my hands. I wasn't walking away from this boy. It didn't matter how badly it could end, or how much trouble I could get into.

Because to have him around, even if only this weird sort of friendship we had going, that would be worth any bad outcomes.

But then there was the fact that he'd gotten too close the other day.

He saw a bruise. On *my* skin.

Somehow, my best lie was the 'I fell down the stairs' line, and I was shocked he even let it go.

That might have had something to do with the fact I was practically sobbing in his arms, but he… he was lovely.

He didn't make fun of me for crying.

He did the opposite.

He comforted me, and gave me advice that clearly came from experience. Nobody could understand grief that deeply if it wasn't affecting them every day.

But for a girl like me, opening up didn't come so easily.

Plus, my situation was more complicated than that.

I knew Archie would believe me if I told him about my home situation, but he wouldn't be able to know that fact and do nothing.

He would tell the police, and we would be thrown into foster care.

I knew foster care would be far better then what we had now, but we would be split up. Me and my brothers.

To an outside perspective, it would seem silly. Staying in an abusive home simply so you don't lose touch with your siblings.

But I think when you're raised in a home like ours, you form a different sort of connection.

A very different, and very bloody complicated one.

"You holding up okay?" Archie asked then, snapping me out of my thoughts.

"I will be," I whispered, twirling a piece of grass around my finger.

"Yeah, I think you will." He nodded. "We should get back to the others."

Putting an end to the lingering look we shared, I smiled weakly. "Yeah. Yeah, we should."

Chapter seventeen
April 27th 2004

SAVANNAH

It was our first day back after Easter break, and the radiating excitement was palpable.

"Did you hear the basketball and cheer tournament got confirmed?" Josie announced, auburn hair catching the wind as she practically flung herself into her designated chair at our lunch table.

"Really?" Danny asked with about as much enthusiasm as a lazy golden retriever as he took a bite of his sandwich.

Archie, who had recently started joining us for lunch, chimed in next. "Coach told us at practice. You didn't show up. Again."

Danny scoffed and mumbled something about 'priorities' between chews.

"You know who did show up?" Liv waggled her eyebrows, looking right at me. "My girl, Savannah."

Yeah, I had done that.

Coach told me I was better than half the girls on the team.

I wasn't sure I believed him, but it was nice to see somebody have hope in me.

While my starting cheer was almost as unexpected as me beginning to trust Archie Bennett this year, I'd honestly enjoyed it.

Excluding the fact that meant I was expected at the cheer tournament.

Some people weren't able to just *go*.

I wasn't sure where or when the trip was, but I was almost positive I'd be absent.

Unless *he* wasn't home.

"I'm proud of you," Liv added with a smile, as bright and warm as ever. "You killed it."

I smiled back, small but real. It felt good hearing that from someone who wasn't a teacher or Coach lying out of politeness.

In a sense, joining cheer felt like regaining some sort of control over my life, considering I couldn't do that anywhere else.

I understood now why a lot of Jayden's time was taken up by basketball. It was comforting.

"Are you coming on the trip then?" Josie asked, her voice casual but her eyes trained on me like she already knew the answer.

I hesitated. "I don't know."

She tilted her head. "Why not?"

I shrugged, playing it off like it wasn't a big deal. "Might be busy."

Josie and Liv exchanged a look. Not subtle. One of those quiet conversations you only hear if you know how to listen. They knew I wasn't busy.

Archie, oblivious as ever, shoved the rest of his protein bar in his mouth and said, "It's gonna be great. Three days, free food, tournaments and hotel rooms."

The others grinned in argument.

"I'll ask," I blurted out suddenly, cutting through the chatter before I could talk myself out of it. "My mum, I mean. I'll ask her tonight."

Liv squeezed my hand under the table.

Josie gave me a small nod, like she was proud but didn't want to make a big deal of it in front of everyone.

A barely visible smile appeared on Izzie's face.

That was enough. For Izzie, that was everything.

I had to try.

I owed them at least that.

Archie's head snapped up, suddenly intrigued. "You should come."

He said it like it was simple. Like it made sense.

Like I'd never flinched around him and he'd never seen that bruise.

I looked up, and he was already looking at me.

He didn't look at me the way he looked at everyone else. He hadn't for a while.

The way his green eyes gazed at me, like they could see right through me, it was intense. But it was a soft intensity. Steady.

His foot brushed against mine under the table.

Was that on purpose?

Was I supposed to say something?

I didn't move.

And God, I would have moved if he were any other boy.

But that was the problem.

He wasn't any other boy.

He was *Archie*.

And I'd come to learn that name meant more than any other.

"Yeah?" I said, keeping my voice neutral, eyes locked on his.

"Yeah." He held my gaze easily. "It'll be better if you're there."

It wasn't flirty.

It was worse.

It was honest.

I looked away first.

Liv was smiling like she knew something I didn't, and Josie was doing that thing where she blinked real slow like she was physically restraining herself from saying, *finally*.

I wasn't sure if that was right, though.

I knew I was letting him get closer. Maybe too close.

I knew that.

But I couldn't stop myself now.

However it happened, Archie Bennett had managed to sit at the back of my mind every day. Well, the fore point.

I wasn't sure what this feeling was, but what I did know was that I'd never felt it before. I think it was the feeling I'd been running from my whole life.

It was ridiculous. I'd only known him for a few months.

But in those few months, he'd become the center of my thoughts in a way I didn't know how to untangle. Maybe it wasn't possible.

Archie Bennett was supposed to be another guy who made stupid jokes and laughed at all the wrong moments. One of those dickhead guys who only wanted you once and that was it.

But that wasn't him.

He wasn't the type of person everyone made him out to be.

He had a way of pulling me in, even when every bone in my body told me to run before I got hurt.

I don't think he knew it, but that had never, *never* happened to me before.

Usually, I had no problem with leaving. Actually, I was always leaving. Even with my friends. It didn't matter that I physically showed up. Because mentally? I was already halfway to another country.

But with him? It felt like I was cracked wide open but still desperately holding on with trembling hands.

Whether he knew or not, he was the first guy I'd ever felt anything for after spending my whole life depriving myself of happiness.

I didn't know what the feeling was, but I knew it was good.

And I knew all too well how quickly good things could be ripped from your hands.

I suddenly stood up, trying to shake off the weight of the tension in the air. "Well, I guess I'll see you guys tomorrow," I said, the words feeling too light for the way my heart was thumping in my chest.

Liv shot me a look. One that said *I'm here for you forever.*

I walked away from the lunch table with my head spinning.

What the hell was happening to me?

I had bigger things to worry about.

My whole life was a crumbling mess and I was thinking about a boy. A boy!

I never understood it. How with such a hard life, Jayden could find it in himself to fall in love.

That wasn't to say there hadn't been many ups and downs between him and Caroline, because there certainly had, but he did it regardless. He found someone worth staying for, and did exactly that.

I wasn't sure if I was brave enough to do that.

Archie was beginning to mean too much. I didn't know how to explain it.

I didn't want to explain it.

And yet, I *couldn't* stop thinking about it.

Why did it matter so much to me what he thought? Why did I care so much when I *shouldn't*?

Because I didn't trust anyone that easily.

I didn't let people in.

But somehow, Archie had found a way through the walls I'd built.

And I wasn't sure if I should be mad at him for it or grateful. Slap him, or kiss him.

I didn't want to let him any closer. I knew I shouldn't.

But every time he looked at me, I realised I was getting *too* used to that softness in his gaze.

God, there was no way this could end well for me.

✦

I'd been staring at the back of my mum's head in the kitchen for ten minutes.

It was only a damn school trip.

I hated how much more that meant in a family like this.

All I wanted was to live a little bit. To be a normal teenager. To go out with my friends and not feel the constant dread of going home.

Because home was the place I should have felt most comfortable.

Finally, I cleared my throat, my voice cracking a little. "Mum?"

Her head snapped up, face as pale as ever. "Are you okay?"

I hated that being her first question.

I folded my arms, hugging myself a little tighter than usual. "I'm… well, I joined cheer."

"You joined cheer?" Her lifeless brown eyes widened slightly.

I nodded once. "There's this basketball and cheer tournament next week. It's…um, it goes for a couple nights. Everyone's going."

The silence that followed made the air feel too thick. The knife paused mid-cut, and I could see the hesitation flicker across her face.

"Savannah…" She put the knife down slowly, voice almost too careful. "Do you think that's a good idea?"

My eyes darted around, making sure my father hadn't arrived home from the bar.

"I think I'm sick of asking myself that question about *everything*," I admitted, voice barely above a whisper. "I know you love him, mum. And you feel you have some twisted sort of dedication towards him. But please. I never ask you for anything."

She bit down on her lip. "Savannah, you know what he will do."

"Hit me?" I scoffed, raising an eyebrow. "He does that anyway, mum. To you. To me. To the boys. What difference does it make anymore?"

Her gaze softened, just a little. She turned away for a moment, staring out the window, like she was deep in thought. Maybe she was reflecting on the guilt, or the fact that she'd brought me into a world I never asked to be a part of and kept me from experiencing the rare positives. But she looked *sad*.

When she spoke again, her voice was quieter. "You know I don't like to betray your father."

I could feel the distance between us growing, even though we were standing only a few feet apart. I wanted to reach out, to make her see how much this meant to me, how important it was for me to feel like I wasn't trapped by everything that happened before.

But she was... God, she was so far gone.

She was a ghost of the woman I knew as my mother.

And I knew she was a victim. Truly, I understood that. I hated that her life from sixteen years old consisted of abuse and cruelty. But she went and put that life onto five children. That made her a villain, too.

"Please," I whispered, finally meeting her eyes. "I'm asking *you*. I'm not asking him. This isn't about him. You have a mind outside of him, too."

She sighed again, a long exhale that felt like a release. "When is it?"

"Next Tuesday."

"How many nights?"

I sighed. "Two. I know it's a lot, but I just can't–"

"Fine."

I stopped rambling, tilting my head in disbelief. "What?"

"I said fine, Savannah." Mum nodded firmly. "Your father got angry this morning and decided to stay with his cousins for a while. If he comes back while you're away, we'll come up with something."

"Thank you," I said quietly, rushing upstairs before she had a chance to change her mind.

While I hated the idea of leaving Jayden here with the boys, he'd done the same thing to me last year.

We were both perfectly capable of taking care of them, and understood how desperately you need breaks when you're living in a house as dysfunctional as ours.

Once I reached my room, I slid my phone out from the compartment beneath my single bed, dialing Liv's number.

"Savannah?" Her voice came through choppy on the other end, but quickly cleared up. "Did you ask about the trip?"

I nodded before realising she couldn't see me. "She said yes."

Liv went silent for a moment. "She really did?"

"Yeah." I smiled. "Yeah, she did."

Freedom.

Even if only for a few nights.

It meant *everything*.

"Hey, Savannah?" Liv whispered, and I could hear her curiosity through the phone.

"Yeah?" I replied, still smiling to myself.

She was quiet for a moment before asking, "Do you like him?"

I froze, smile turning into a frown. "Who?"

She scoffed in disbelief. "You *know* who."

Sigh...

I did.

Was it that obvious?

"Yeah," I breathed, voicing it aloud for the first time. "I think I really do."

"I know," she said, voice soft. Understanding. "You're in pretty deep, huh?"

"Yeah," I agreed, rolling onto my side. "I'm so stupid."

"No," she immediately argued. "You are smart, and you are brave. You're sixteen years old and you've been through unimaginable things, yet you're still here. No boy can take that from you."

I swallowed, extra thankful for my best friend tonight. "Thank you."

Chapter eighteen
May 4th 2004

ARCHIE

The bus reeked of salt and sweat and the weirdly specific scent of sour patch kids.

Sav was three rows ahead.

Not that I was counting.

She had her earbuds in, head tilted just slightly toward the window, the sun catching the edge of her cheekbone.

As usual, Liv was talking her ear off, hands flying everywhere, and Sav just nodded, smiled once. One of those subtle ones that you barely notice unless you're watching too closely. I probably was.

I always seemed to be when Sav was the girl in question.

"Do ya reckon they'll let me share a room with Livvy?" Theo asked, frowning.

"Not after last time," I snickered.

"That was *not* my fault."

"You lit a smoke and set off the fire alarm."

Theo scowled. "That smoke alarm was very fucking sensetive."

I laughed, because it was impossible not to.

"You better hope Coach doesn't find out you're already planning room swaps," I said.

He smirked, kicking his feet up on the seat in front of us. "What Coach doesn't know won't kill him."

Except Coach *always* knew. Somehow. Like he had us all chipped.

I'd stopped questioning it, though.

Because Coach *had* raised us. Raised *me.*

He was my Coach since third grade, and had followed our team into high school a few years ago. He'd been there for it all.

The good *and* the bad.

The bus began to slow then, a fancy hotel with a circular driveway and a fountain coming into view.

Everyone started chatting again, untangling their earbuds and hopping up from their seats.

We'd been on this bus for three hours, and the arrival was a moment that should have felt exciting. But it didn't.

Because Sav finally turned around in her seat.

Her eyes landed on me for half a second.

Half a second.

That's all it ever was.

And then she looked past me like I wasn't even there.

But that was the thing.

Even when she wasn't looking at me at all… I *always* saw her.

And I knew she saw me too.

"Hate to ruin the party, but quit staring at her," Theo muttered, shaking his head. "It's really obvious. And really fucking strange."

"What?" I looked at him, tearing my eyes away from Sav. "I wasn't staring at anyone."

"Do you know what you could do?"

"What?"

He pretended to think for a moment. "Speak to her. It's always a good option."

I sighed.

Not because he was wrong, but because he was so painfully right.

For the first time in our eleven years of friendship, he had the right answer. Not me.

But it was usually much easier than this.

I didn't struggle to talk to girls, and I sure as hell didn't watch them from afar, hoping they let me in more.

Didn't used to, anyway.

◆

Theo flopped on the left side of the bed as soon as we entered our room.

"Not even a discussion?" I asked, kicking my shoes off.

"Nope." He grinned proudly. "If I'm on this side, you'll get murdered first."

I shook my head, a chuckle escaping my lips. "You're such a girl."

"No." He pointed a finger at me, a determined look on his face. "Livvy always gets the left side. It's my turn."

"For the record, I still find it strange that you two sleep in the same bed every night," I told him.

"Why?" He tilted his head, genuinely confused. "She's my best friend."

'Bullshit," I chuckled, shaking my head.

Theo rolled his eyes. "Guess who's next door?"

I didn't have to ask. The laughter was already seeping through the wall. Light, bright, too damn familiar.

Sav.

And Liv.

Right bloody there.

I groaned, leaning against the wall. "Right there?"

"Uh huh." He smirked, sliding down beside me. "So, are you gonna talk about it?"

I cocked a brow. "What?"

"You clearly like the girl," he said casually, gesturing to the other wall, the thin one separating us and the girls. "I knew that. But it's been months and you're still on the same girl." He shrugged. "That never happens. You're the definition of a man whore."

"Excuse me?"

He chuckled to himself. "Sorry. Are you not a man whore anymore?"

"Maybe I'm evolving," I snickered.

"Evolving?" He frowned. "That's what we're going with?"

I sighed, leaning my head against the wall. "I don't know."

"There's clearly something different about this one. Everyone knows that, but now you're seeing it too," he said, mask of humour completely gone. "You don't look at her the way you did the rest of them."

"Maybe I don't," I admitted, drumming my fingers against my knee. "Fuck if I know."

"Don't." He raised an eyebrow, slow and skeptical. "Not with her, anyway. You care about Savannah. Why is that so hard to admit?"

"You're one to talk."

"Hey. me and Livvy do perfectly fine at keeping it platonic." He held up his hands. "It's about you this time."

Rolling my eyes, I nodded. "Yeah, it's about me.'

"I never expected to be the one giving you advice on girls." He grinned to himself, nodding in approval.

"Do not give me advice."

"You know you can't stop me," Theo snickered. "Now, you're my best friend. But Savannah has always been Livvy's. She's a sister to me. So I won't hesitate to cut your dick off if you hurt the girl."

Fucking hell.

If Theo was being serious about this? It mattered more than I cared to admit.

"That wasn't friendly advice." I glared at him, rubbing the back of my neck.

He laughed under his breath. "Alright. Well, I think that if you care about her... and I mean truly care about her, you should tell her."

"I barely know her."

"You do."

"But I've only-"

"You know her," he repeated slowly. "Whether it's friendship or more, look out for the girl." He paused. "God knows somebody needs to."

My head snapped up, immediately alarmed. "What do you mean?"

"Savannah has always been a lovely girl. Always," he told me, but I already knew that. Too well. "Her family, though? Not so lovely."

Yeah, I figured as much.

That wasn't to say I thought they were bad people, but she had hardly mentioned her parents. Maybe they cared so much that it became controlling.

"What's wrong with them?" I asked, hoping he knew more than I did.

"I don't know," he admitted with a sigh. "But I know Livvy's dad never allowed her to go over there."

"But they're best friends." I frowned, confused.

"Yeah, but Savannah always went to Livvy's," he explained. "That's why I've known her for so long."

"She didn't go to primary with us?" I questioned, frowning. "I didn't pay much attention."

He scratched at his jaw, thinking. "Nah. Public one down the road. Family couldn't afford it."

Shit.

When I dropped her home, there were definitely signs the family struggled with money.

Not anything big, but the house was quite run down and not exactly in the loveliest area of Ridgewood.

"How did she get into Ridgewood then?" I questioned.

"Scholarship."

Huh.

Then there was a knock.

I jumped up, heading straight for the door.

Of course, it flung open before I had the chance to do it myself.

Danny appeared in the doorway, barging in unannounced.

"Hey." He smirked. "We're all going down to the pool."

"Why?" I asked, lifting a brow. "What time is it?"

"10pm," he said, waving to Theo who hadn't bothered to get up. "But there's a really fucking big pool and it sounds better than staying in."

I sighed, glancing over at Theo who, of course, was nodding rapidly. "Fine."

"Good." Danny stuck his thumbs up mockingly. "You need to loosen up anyway."

He wasn't wrong.

✦

The music pulsed low and steady by the pool.

Danny was right.

There were at least sixty of us down here, and it was no struggle to fit.

Laughter flared from the diving board as Theo cannonballed in, soaking three girls who had definitely not planned on swimming tonight.

The whole cheer squad other than Olivia and Sav were down here.

But I wasn't watching any of them.

I hadn't watched any of them in a long time.

The moment I saw Sav for the first time... that was it. For me, anyway. All the girls, and the parties, and the bars? I lost all interest.

But this was a whole lot bloody harder than a new girl every week.

Yeah, spending all my time obsessing over one girl I could never possibly deserve may not have been the smartest idea, and I would have stopped it if I could.

But there were no questions.

It was weird. It was almost like each time she talked to me, something settled inside of me. Like the more time that went by of knowing her, the more I wondered how I lived without for so long.

I was addicted to a girl I may never have.

Christ, that was pathetic.

"Cap!" Riley Campbell approached me, eyes clean and sober compared to the way he usually looked. "What's the play tomorrow? Anything changed?"

I nodded once. "If we swap you and Billy, we can… uh…"

I trailed off, blinking hard.

Because Sav had just shown up.

Her bikini was black, minimal, tied like an afterthought at her hips. She shook her braid out over one shoulder as if unaware of every single eye on her.

Fuck. she didn't even realise how many people were watching.

"Capiel!" I shouted, glaring at the guy who was watching Sav. "Get over here."

And he did.

Smart plan, fucker.

"You're benched for the first half of tomorrow's game," I told him firmly, my attention flicking to Riley. "You'll go on instead."

Riley nodded, but Mason Capiel frowned.

"Come on, Cap-"

"That is an order," I told him, voice raising slightly. "And keep your eyes the fuck off Savannah Grey."

"What?" He raised an eyebrow, a grin stretching across his face. "Are ya kidding?"

"I'm serious," I continued. "I can have ya benched for the whole season if that's how you want to do this. Or, we can do it my way. Keep your eyes off her."

"Alright, Cap. Christ," he muttered under his breath, making his way back to his friends.

Yeah, that wasn't very rational of me.

But fuck.

He was really looking at her.

I wasn't about to allow that.

Not trusting myself to watch her for too long, I turned my head away.

Coach was standing by the edge of the pool. Not smiling, but not frowning either. He was just watching. Just *present.*

Present for me, I realised.

He was sixty. He had no reason to stand by the pool, watching a group of teenagers fuck around.

But he was.

He proved time and again that he would continue to show up for me, whether I protested or not. I'd stopped doing that, though.

I'd let him show up.

He knew that was my way of saying *thank you.*

Sav slipped into the pool then, catching my eye like she was programmed to do exactly that.

"You're staring," she tilted her head, slicking her braid back with both hands.

I laughed quietly. "You make it hard not to."

She frowned. "Don't flirt with me."

"Why not?" I asked, suddenly confident.

"I don't…" She thought for a moment, adjusting the strap of her bikini. "I don't know."

I nodded. "Well, alright then."

"Alright then," she repeated quietly, a small smile playing on her full lips. "I've been on the cheer team for what… a week? And I'm already doing a tournament. That's scary."

"No, it's brave," I told her, smiling back. "You'll do great. The teams lucky to have ya."

That earned me a more natural grin. "Thanks."

"Uh huh."

"You good?" She asked a few moments later, not missing a beat.

"Yeah," I said, more to myself than her."Yeah, I think I am."

Chapter nineteen
May 5th 2004

SAVANNAH

The crowd was already unbelievably loud by the time we arrived on the sidelines.

The boys had just won their first game of the tournament.

Now it was our turn.

My turn.

As my eyes scanned the crowd, all I could wonder was how I'd ended up here. I mean, a few months ago I wouldn't have even considered joining the team. But now? I was *performing*.

I never thought I'd fit in well with cheer.

But it was almost like I could stop pretending for a few moments.

It wasn't an act. It was *me*. Freedom.

Then my eyes landed on Archie.

He was in the crowd with the other boys, half engaged in a conversation.

But his eyes were staring right back at me.

I looked down a half-second later, adjusting the straps of my uniform.

I always caught myself watching him.

But I couldn't help it.

Each time he met my eyes, my heart skipped a beat before I could stop it.

I was here to play. To focus.

But how could I focus when he was here?

Archie had been in the crowd of many of these tournaments. Back when I was another girl on the bleachers.

But back then, his eyes never stayed on one person.

They flickered from girl to girl.

But today? Today, they were entirely on me.

God, that affected me more than it should have.

I was in too deep, I realised, admitting it to myself for the first time. Too deep in this. Too deep in *him*.

It was terrifying.

While I'd spent most of my life afraid of boys and men, it wasn't like that now.

Not with *him*.

I didn't have any experience to go off, but I figured I wouldn't be one of those girls who could fall in love, and still be capable of falling out of it.

The reason I ran from people was because I would get so easily attached otherwise. Like a baby to their mother, you know?

But it wasn't fair of me to get attached now.

There were too many factors.

What if he found out how much I hid? Would he still stay? Or would he leave? What would I prefer? And what about me? Would I stay if he found out?

I looked up again, just as Archie caught my eye. There was no smile this time, no teasing glint. Just a steady look. It was… soft.

It hit me in the chest like a sudden wave of warmth, and for a moment, all the noise of the tournament disappeared. The crowd faded, the pressure dissolved.

For the first time in days, I took a breath without thinking about it.

Before I could fall deeper into my thoughts, Coach clapped me on the shoulder. "You okay?"

I nodded.

"You're a fighter, Grey." He shot me a wink of reassurance. "You've got this. Don't let cheer or anything else take that away from you."

"Thanks," I whispered, grateful for his comfort.

Just when I thought he was done, he turned back around. "And, Grey? Don't give up on the boy."

My eyes widened.

And he was gone.

What?

I blinked after him, still half-frozen in place. *Don't give up on the boy*? What did that even mean? Had he seen something? Had *everyone* seen something?

The thought made my chest tighten, and I quickly turned away before my face could give me away too.

No, no, no.

Stop overthinking, Savannah.

A part of me wanted to laugh. I didn't do things like this. I didn't catch feelings. I didn't fall into boys' eyes and hope they caught me.

I didn't need saving. Didn't need fixing.

At least, that's what I thought.

But really…would it be so bad to let him get closer? Maybe. But I was beginning to think that was a risk worth taking.

Shit.

I was *falling* for him. Hard and fast.
Dangerous.

I shook it off and walked back toward the bench, the ache in my chest sharp and sudden. I needed to snap out of it. Focus. Cheer. That was what I was here for. Not... whatever this was.

Then the whistles blew, signaling the beginning of our performance.

So I did it. Put my attention where it belonged.

Even if my mind was drifting to places it had no business residing in.

✦

"So Ridgewood is in the lead for both so far," Josie announced over a bite of steak. "If Mount Eli loses their game against the other team tonight, we've won.

"Yeah." Archie nodded from beside me, grinning to himself. "We've got this. Easily. The other teams are shit."

Theo snorted at something Liv said, lazily draping an arm over her shoulder.

Yeah, this 'celebratory dinner' at midnight was feeling a lot like a family dinner.

Well, a dinner in normal households.

It was lovely, though. The kind of lovely that made my chest ache a little.

Because if life was like this all the time, I might have had a chance of happiness.

I felt like that chance had been stolen from me at birth.

"Coach texted," Archie said, smiling. "We won it."

The table erupted into conversation then, laughter and cheers about how they always knew we'd end up with the win.

I was still surprised I'd gotten through it without breaking.

Archie sipped his lemonade, eyes half-lidded in amusement at something Theo had mumbled. His foot nudged mine under the table again.

He had done that too many times for me to mistake it as an accident this time.

I should've pulled away. I didn't.

Instead, I shifted just slightly. Leaned into the contact like it was something safe.

Maybe it was.

After all, I'd grown up around danger. I knew danger like the back of my hand. But Archie? He didn't give me that same fear I felt around most people.

He was nice. Genuine.

My stomach fluttered as I pushed another piece of broccoli around my plate, pretending I didn't notice the weight of too many unspoken words hanging between us. Pretending this was all just friendly. Pretending that I wasn't unraveling a little every time he looked my way.

A few minutes later, Theo was somehow halfway into a story about the 'downfall' of his evil parrot Fred, and Liv was whispering something into his ear that made his grin widen into something obnoxious.

I wanted that joy. Safety. Comfort.

I wasn't sure how I felt about Archie, but I knew it should have felt wrong.

Yet, somehow, It felt so damn right.

All of this did.

And I realised that if I was brave enough, this could be my life. I *could* have love and stability.

But it was one of those things that was easier said than done.

"This food's terrible," Archie muttered a few minutes later, green eyes locking on mine. "Wanna come to the vending machine with me?"

I hesitated before saying, "Okay."

The hallway was empty, only lit by the faint blue glow of the vending machine, casting shadows across the floor.

He hummed, then studied the machine like it held the meaning of life. "So what's the move? Chocolate? Chips? Mystery gummy… things?"

"None of it," I admitted. "I don't really need food."

Archie looked at me then. Really *looked*.

"Yeah," he said quietly. "Me neither."

It went silent for a moment.

Then, quieter, "Savannah."

I turned toward him.

He was staring at the floor like the words were heavier than he wanted them to be. "I didn't mean to make things weird at dinner. I don't know if I did. But I'm just… fuck. Sorry."

"You didn't."

"I feel like I did."

"You didn't," I repeated, firmer this time.

He blew out a shaky breath. "Good."

I nodded simply, turning my gaze back to the vending machine.

That was easier than staring into his eyes.

"You're really far away," Archie whispered.

Confused, I whispered, "I'm right here."

"You are. Physically," he replied. "But it feels like you're a whole world away."

His words felt like a dagger to the chest. A harsh reminder of how far I kept myself from everything. From him.

I didn't say anything at first.

There were many things I could've said. Should've said. But they were all stuck on the tip of my tongue.

I pressed my fingertips to the edge of the vending machine, willing myself to stay calm.

"I don't mean to be," I said finally. "I don't know. I've just… always been that way."

"Why?" he asked gently.

I looked at him then, and it was a mistake. His face was open in that boyish, earnest way that made me want to tell him everything. And that terrified me.

Because there was far too much on the line.

For me. For him.

He had his whole life set out for him. Welcoming him into the mess of my life would take that away. Keep him stuck here just like me.

"Does it matter?"

"It matters," he quickly confirmed.

"If people don't really get in, they can't leave," I heard myself admit truthfully. "It's easier like that."

He sighed. "Well, that works for me. Because I don't plan on going anywhere."

"Archie-"

"Sav," he cut me off. "You don't need to say anything. But I plan to stick around, whether you're ready to admit that you want me to or not."

I swallowed hard.

Somehow, all I could choke out was, "You scare me."

He didn't flinch or look surprised. Just nodded, like maybe he understood.

"Yeah. You scare me too."

My chest cracked open just a little.

So I did the only thing I could at that moment.

I reached for his hand.

And he let me.

Chapter twenty

May 10th 2004

ARCHIE

"Do you always take this long to get in the car?" I asked, grinning.

Sav rolled her eyes, but there was a smile playing on her lips. "I'm deciding whether I trust your driving."

"You've been in my car before."

"True," she agreed with a soft laugh, finally sliding into the passenger seat.

I shut the driver's side door and started the engine.

She glanced at me once we hit the main road, eyebrows raised slightly like she was waiting for me to make a wrong turn or slam the brakes.

I smirked but didn't say anything. Let her watch.

School dragged on forever today, and training was bloody exhausting. Maybe I'd never admit it, but time with Sav was exactly what I needed.

A few blocks passed before she leaned back in her seat and let out a slow breath, like she was relaxing on purpose.

"Thanks for driving me home again," she finally said. "Sorry it's out of your way."

I waved a hand in the air, dismissing her worries. "No need to thank me."

That earned me a smile.

"Are you okay?" I heard myself ask.

Her head snapped up, grey eyes looking right through me. "You always ask me that."

"I always wonder that," I answered without hesitation.

She nodded slowly, like she was trying to understand why somebody cared.

"Well, I'm okay.' She smiled, fiddling with the hem of her blazer. "Thanks."

I raised an eyebrow, but let it slide.

That's when the rain started.

My jaw clenched. My body tensed.

"What's wrong?" Sav asked, glancing at the window then at my face. "Archie? Are you okay?"

I pulled onto the side of the road immediately, not saying a word.

"The car crash," she whispered, eyes widening in realisation once we parked. "Oh, God."

"It was raining," I confirmed quietly. "And I think it might have been my fault."

She tilted her head, eyes widening. "Why do you think that?"

"It was my game we were going to," I said honestly, flinching at the memories flashing through my mind. "We knew it was dangerous to drive in the rain. But I… I didn't want to miss my game. Now… now, I guess I can't drive while it's raining."

I wasn't sure why I was telling her this.

But it was all coming out before I could stop it.

"That doesn't make it your fault," she assured me gently.

I knew that.

At least, I should have known that.

"Do you remember when you were talking to me about Marlee?" She asked, voice soft and caring. "Well, we're gonna switch sides now."

I managed a weak laugh, leaning back in my chair. "Alright."

"I'm not very good at this stuff," she admitted, frowning to herself. "But I'm gonna try, because if I know anything, it's that you couldn't have changed what happened that night." She offered me a tiny, barely visible smile.

"But what if-"

"You. Couldn't. Have. Known," she said slowly. "That night was *not* your fault."

Maybe I couldn't have known. But I should have. God, I should have.

"If I'd been willing to miss one game…" I ran a hand down my face frustratedly, glancing over at her. "Only one, and they'd still be alive."

Sav didn't interrupt. She let me talk, and that meant more than anything she could've said.

"That night is on a constant fucking loop in my mind."

She reached out slowly, like she didn't want to startle me. Her hand landed on mine, warm and firm.

"You don't talk about it." She held my gaze, searching my eyes. "Do you?"

I sighed. "Everyone has their own shit going on. I don't want to dump this on you, either."

"You're not," she argued, shaking her head. "You're sharing it. Opening up. That's different. That's… really brave."

She rubbed her thumb against my knuckles absentmindedly, and I let her.

"I'm glad you felt okay to tell me," she whispered. "I thought I'd be better at this."

"You're doing great," I managed, and I meant it more than I expected to. "You know you can talk to me as well, right?"

"I know that," she murmured, but I'm not sure she even convinced herself.

We fell into a silence then, but it felt more like breathing space.

"She left letters," Sav blurted out a few moments later. "Marlee, I mean."

Yeah, I'd heard about that.

I remembered each of the boys receiving theirs last year. Nobody had ever found the courage to read them, though.

God, that only made the situation more fucked up.

Marlee knew she was out of time, and still spent her last hours on earth writing letters to her friends. The people who stayed.

It was really bloody screwed up.

"I know," I replied with a nod. "Did you ever… read it?'

She shook her head. "I tried." Her voice cracked just slightly, and I saw her jaw tense the way it always did when she was trying not to cry.

Silence.

"It didn't feel real," she admitted after a beat. "Reading her handwriting, knowing she touched the paper…" she shook her head, eyes blinking hard. "I couldn't do it."

Fuck.

She was really opening up to me.

I wasn't sure if this would ever happen.

I didn't speak. I don't think I needed to.

Sav brushed a light brown wave behind her ear, letting her small hands fall to her lap. "She wasn't perfect. Marlee. People talk about her like she was either an angel or a devil. She wasn't either of those things. She was stubborn and impulsive, but she was never bad. She was always loyal and trusting. *Too* trusting."

There were a million things I could have said. But she didn't need me to speak.

She needed me to stay. To listen.

I'd be damned if that wasn't exactly what I planned to do.

"I know you didn't know her well, but she truly was wonderful." She smiled at the memory, soft and sharp at the same time. "But she would've liked you."

I swallowed, unsure how to respond to a ghost's approval.

"I didn't even know her," I said, the guilt eating away at me even now.

"You didn't need to." She shrugged. "You were always kind to Marlee. And now, you're one of the only people who don't talk about her as gossip. She'd appreciate that."

We sat with that for a while.

The rain began to slow down, calming the ache in my chest.

"The rains passed," Sav whispered.

I nodded. "Right."

Maybe it was selfish, but I wanted to keep her here forever. Completely safe. With *me*.

Christ, this girl was fucking with my mind more and more every day, and she didn't even know it.

I turned the engine back on, pulling onto the main road.

We passed a few more blocks in silence, the only noise being the occasional breeze of wind or Sav shifting around in her seat.

Finally, she broke the silence. "Thanks for… being nice to me."

I chuckled, the tension in my shoulders easing."Well, I try."

The rain had mostly vanished, the streets still wet but calm. The entire town always felt a little quieter after rain, like it was holding its breath.

I slowed as we approached her house.

"You good?" I asked as I pulled into the familiar cracked driveway that always made me a little uncomfortable.

She gave me a smile, but it was less natural this time. More practiced. "Yeah. Thanks again, Archie."

I nodded as she carefully slid open the passenger door.

"I'll be seeing you," I said, catching her just before she got out. This time, her smile softened to something true.

I watched her retreating frame as she headed to the front door, an involuntary smile stretching across my face.

Nothing changed.

I knew that. I'd known from the start that things may never change.

Still, the certainty settled into my chest like a reminder that she *was* worth it.

I was unsure of the reasons, but it was obvious: she was afraid. Almost as if she was waiting for the rug to be pulled out.

But that didn't mean I was going anywhere. I was prepared to weather every storm, open every slammed door as long as she stayed. It didn't matter. I'd always be here, waiting, no matter how long it could take.

Chapter twenty one

May 14th 2004

SAVANNAH

"Happy birthday." I grinned, hugging Izzie against all her protests.

I stepped inside, people scattered across both floors of Izzie and Danny's family mansion that never failed to impress me.

"Thanks," she said casually, gesturing for me to step inside.

I could barely hear myself talking over the loud mix of blaring music and laughter, but it didn't matter.

It was Izzie and Dannys's sixteenth birthday.

One party I couldn't skip out on, no matter how many punches I endured just to be allowed out.

Their last birthday hadn't exactly been one for the scrapbook. Especially for Izzie.

It was her first birthday since Marlee's death. The one day she wanted her best friend around most. Celebrating these milestones were still hard for me, and I could only imagine how it must have felt for Izzie.

So I didn't hesitate to show up.

I followed her through the crowd, my eyes catching on flashes of glittering dresses, half-finished drinks, and the occasional couple pressed too close in dark corners. It was the kind of chaos Izzie used to thrive in. Maybe she still did. Or maybe, like me, she was just pretending tonight.

I realised it then: I barely knew her anymore.

All I knew was that underneath the facade, she was still the same girl I once knew. Even if nobody else saw that.

Other than that? She was a mystery.

And I wanted my friend back.

We reached the back patio, where the music wasn't quite as deafening. She grabbed a bottle of something alcoholic from the eski and handed it to me without asking. "You look nice," she said, avoiding my eyes.

She always did that. Like she was afraid of what she could find if she looked into them for too long. I think everyone did that around me. Everyone but Archie.

"You sound surprised," I replied mid-laugh, popping the lid off my drink.

She gave me a small, half amused smile. "Just not used to seeing you in dresses." Her midnight blue eyes scanned my body for a moment before finally looking me in the eyes. "Yellow is definitely your colour."

Yellow certainly was *not* my colour, but it was the only dress I owned. Courtesy of Caroline.

"Well, it's a special occasion." I nudged her shoulder lightly. "Only the best for my favourite twin."

She rolled her eyes. "Don't let Danny hear you say that. He's impossible enough as it is."

I smiled, sipping my drink slowly. "I'll take my chances."

Her laugh was short but real. And it hit me how long it had been since I'd seen her like this. Alive. Not fully, and definitely not like she used to be, but it was enough to remind me why I stayed. Why I *always* did, and always planned to.

"She would've loved this," I whispered before I could stop myself.

Izzie's smile faltered just as she nodded. "Yeah, she would have." Her voice cracked, and she turned away, pretending to fuss over the eski.

I reached out and touched her wrist gently. "I'm glad you're here, Izzie."

She looked at me. Really looked. And for the first time in a long time, I knew she saw me. Not just as the friend who always stayed, but as the one who remembered. The one who never stopped missing Marlee, too.

But I wasn't only missing Marlee.

Maybe she was the one who stopped breathing, but she wasn't the only one who died that night on the tracks.

Izzie wasn't the same. The Izzie I knew was gone, and maybe, she would never come back.

"I'm glad *you're* here," she whispered back, a shadow of the girl I once knew.

The moment was cut short by Danny's voice booming through the house. "Everybody get your asses inside! It's time!"

Izzie flinched at the volume, her hand quickly wiping under her eyes before anything could fall. "Come on," she muttered, already slipping back into party-host mode.

I followed her through the crowd, dodging groups of boys and every random girl who attempted talking to Izzie. She did the same, but with a scowl on her face.

Danny stood on the top step, using a red cup as a microphone. "Okay, shut up for two minutes!" he called out, cupping both hands around his mouth."Seriously. If I don't get this speech out, Izzie might actually strangle me while I'm sleeping."

Laughter rolled through the room, echoing from the walls.

Izzie stood next to him now, her smile painfully fixed. I wasn't sure how nobody else saw it. Maybe they did, but wouldn't say it. Everybody was afraid of Izzie now. I think if they knew the girl she used to be, they would feel different.

Billy never gave up hope in her. Right now, he was across the room, watching her intently.

He was *always* watching her. It didn't matter that he was sitting by another girl, a girl who could give him the love he deserved. None of that meant anything when Izzie existed.

Danny's voice softened. "Sixteen. Sure, I can drive now and well, probably crash. But that's not what matters. What matters is the fact that we're still here."

The room fell into silence, nobody even humming along to the music anymore.

"Last year sucked. No sugarcoating it," Danny continued, hand slightly trembling around the cup. "And tonight we wanted to party, yeah, but we also wanted to remember someone who should've been here, singing

Maroon 5 and laughing at Theo's ridiculous jokes."

A few people laughed nervously. Izzie didn't. She was frozen, jaw tight.

I almost thought she would break in front of everybody.

But as I watched her eyes carefully, I could see her fighting it off. It hurt to know she had to fight off the anger. The grief.

But keeping it bottled up really was her only option. Otherwise? All hell would break loose. I knew that all too well.

Danny cleared his throat. "So, raise your glass to Marlee. Our girl. The loudest, brightest pain in the ass. We miss you."

Everyone lifted their drinks in honour. Some shouted her name. A few cried. Izzie blinked rapidly and turned away before anyone could see.

That's when Theo stumbled out from the crowd, half-drunk and glowing like he lived off chaos alone. "To Marlee," he said, clinking his cup against Liv's. "Well, and girls who pretend not to be in love with me."

"Theodore," Liv warned, but I could see her smile.

"What? I'm just saying." He looked her up and down slowly. "You wear red like that and expect me *not* to fantasise?"

A mischievous glint appeared in Liv's eyes as she clapped a hand on his shoulder, broad and unmistakably built. "I fantasised first. Keep up."

Someone snorted. Someone gasped. Theo just looked victorious. Izzie looked like she was going to scream.

I slid closer to her, just in case. Her hands were balled into fists as she glared at Liv's brother, who had, for some reason, insisted on making an appearance tonight.

Izzie turned to me abruptly. "I need air."

I followed her without hesitation as she pushed past a couple making out, and stormed toward the back door, barely holding it together.

"I can't breathe in there," she whispered, voice weaker than ever, hands shaking.

I didn't say anything. Just stood beside her while she folded in on herself, shoulders rising and falling like waves.

Liv came running out the door, breathless. "Theo just tried to toast *us* next and he was- Oh, Izzie."

She froze at the sight of Izzie falling apart.

Without hesitation, Liv wrapped her arms around our friend.

Izzie hesitated for a second, but eventually gave in. Broke down.

It was loud and broken. The kind of crying I could only imagine was worse on *that* night.

"I miss her so much," Izzie choked out a moment later, eyes puffy.

"I know," Liv whispered soothingly, running a gentle hand up and down her back. "We all do."

Adam came into view again, watching the situation unfold through the window.

His expression was unreadable, but it was something that told me Izzie feared him for more reasons that I thought.

I watched Adam from the patio, the way he leaned against the frame of the window like he owned it. His gaze wasn't sympathetic. It wasn't curious, either. It was calculating. Cold

I stepped slightly in front of Izzie without thinking.

Liv didn't notice. She was still murmuring quiet reassurances, her cheek pressed to Izzie's hair.

But I did. And the knot in my stomach twisted tighter.

He didn't move. Just raised the red cup in his hand like a silent toast and turned away, disappearing into the shadows of the house.

Until now, I never understood why the girls were so against him. But that small interaction? That was enough to worry me.

As if flipping a switch, Izzie let go of Liv's hand and exhaled a sharp breath. "Okay. I'm good."

Liv looked doubtful. "Are you sure?"

"No. But I will be."

The door creaked open behind us.

Danny stepped out, his usual cocky smirk replaced with something gentler. "Hey. You okay?"

Izzie nodded once. "Just needed a minute."

"Okay. Well, he's talking about Liv. Things I… don't feel comfortable repeating." He shivered, gaze flicking to Liv. "Can ya go handle him?"

Liv giggled, rolling her eyes. "On it."

Danny laughed, then glanced at me. "You okay?"

I opened my mouth to lie, to say *yeah, fine*, but then I caught Izzie's look. The honest one. The one that said *don't leave me alone with this like everyone else.*

So I shrugged. "Ask me in the morning."

He nodded in understanding, following Liv inside.

"Do you think she blames me?" Izzie asked quietly.

I blinked hard. "Who?"

I knew *who*. I wasn't stupid.

I just really hoped she wasn't carrying that guilt.

"Marlee," she confirmed. "I was there, Savannah. What if I could have saved her? Now I get to live? It's just... it doesn't seem fair."

"It's not fair," I agreed with a small shake of my head. "But not the fact that you're alive. The fact that she isn't." I squeezed harder on her hand, hoping to give her some form of reassurance in the hardest of times. "But Marlee didn't want you to be sad."

"I know that," she said, nodding slowly. "I know."

Silence.

Then, "I should get back inside."

"Are you gonna be okay?" I asked, feeling a surge of worry for my friend, but she was already reaching for the door handle.

"I have a party to host." She blew out a shaky breath, disappearing into the crowd.

I didn't follow. Not right away.

I just stared into the dark, hoping to see Marlee running toward me with that stupidly bright grin.

But she wasn't coming back.

And I would *never* be the same again.

None of us would.

Just as I rose to head inside, I was greeted by the broad, muscular frame I'd learned to look out for. The one I recognised in every crowd.

"Hi, Sav." Just two words, but they hit me somewhere low in the stomach.

"Hi, Archie," I replied, biting nervously on my bottom lip.

His eyes skimmed my body, lingering just long enough to make my breath hitch. "You look wonderful." He gestured vaguely to my dress. "Very wonderful."

Despite my best efforts, I felt a smile stretch across my face. "So do you."

He nodded as we both sat on the bench, close, but not touching. "Was Izzie alright?" He asked, voice soft but sincere. His brows pulled together with genuine concern as he said, "I don't mean to pry, but Danny seemed stressed inside, and he only gets like that when he's worried about his sister."

I nodded in confirmation, tucking a loose strand of hair behind my ear with a swift move of my hand. "Yeah, she just needed a break."

He let out a quiet breath and smiled, reaching for a beer. "How's your night been other than that?"

"It's been okay," I said, frowning a little as the words fell flat.

There was a short pause.

"Hey, Archie?"

"Yeah?" His green eyes immediately locked with mine.

"Do you know Adam Coleman?"

"Olivia's adopted brother?" His brows lifted as he tilted the bottle in his hand, swirling it absently. "Talked to him a few times, but not really. Why?"

I didn't say anything.

Clearly alarmed, his fists clenched at his sides. "Do I need to hurt him?"

I let out a breath of a laugh at his protectiveness. "No, no. I don't really know him. He was just... I don't know."

"Walk me through it," he said, voice steady and curious.

"Okay." I nodded, thinking. "The girls have always been afraid of him. Marlee included. I never understood it, because Liv likes him, and he was always lovely to me. But when Izzie was crying tonight... he was watching. Not in a curious way, I don't think."

His brows furrowed, the crease between his eyes deepening. "Do you think something happened?" he asked, voice rough with concern.

"No," I said honestly. "But I still think there's something off about him."

Archie nodded, sharp and relieved. "Look, if you ever see anything like that again, just say the word."

I gave him a sideways glance. "What, you'll kill him?" I asked, half-laughing.

He chuckled, tilting his head back until his eyes caught the light. "I'll do anything you want me to do."

I glanced at him, the way the moonlight captured his features sending a shiver down my spine. He wasn't joking. Not entirely.

"You say that like it's nothing."

"It's not nothing," he replied, meeting my gaze. "But you're... well, you matter. So, if someone ever made you feel unsafe, I'd want to know."

My throat tightened at his words.

He didn't know it, but I was always unsafe.

Every. Day.

But those words... those very few words. They made me believe that maybe, just maybe, I could confide in him. One day.

"Thank you," I said instead.

"Izzie's lucky," he said suddenly, smiling as he stared at the stars. "To have you."

I looked down at my drink. "She doesn't feel lucky."

"Still," he shrugged. "You're grieving with her, and you're staying. Some people have to go through it on their own."

That got me. Because he said it like he knew what it was like to be one of those people.

And from the small parts of his dad and sisters story that I'd heard? Chances were, he did know.

Very well.

I reached over, touched his hand without thinking. Yeah, being around this boy threw my common sense out the window, but I couldn't fight it anymore. "You can talk to me too, you know? If you ever need to."

His expression shifted, softening just slightly. "That obvious?"

I smiled. "Only a little."

He turned his hand under mine, so our palms met. His skin was warm, steady. Like maybe he *needed* the contact just as much as I did.

The door creaked open behind us again, footsteps crunching softly on the stone.

It was Theo. Of course.

"Thought I'd find you out here." He held a bottle loosely in one hand and had that signature smirk that made girls stupid over him. "You're missing the cake fiasco. Pretty sure Danny lit his sleeve on fire."

Archie sighed, releasing my hand slowly. "We'll be there in a sec."

Theo's eyes flicked between us, eyebrows lifting slightly. "You two good?"

"Fine," I said, a little too quickly.

"You sure?"

Archie stood. "We're good."

Something passed between the two of them then. Not hostility. Some weird friendship thing. Something unsaid.

"Cool. Just checking." Then he disappeared back inside, leaving the night quiet again.

I stood, brushing my hands on my dress. "I should check on Izzie."

"You're not alone, Sav," he called after me. "Not as long as I'm here."

I didn't know what to say to that. So I didn't say anything.

Just walked inside.

Walked away.

But a part of me stayed with him.

Chapter twenty two
May 20th 2004

ARCHIE

I saw her bag before I saw the empty classroom.

She'd clearly left it behind, because it was just sitting there, slouched against the lockers.

Everyone was already gone. Even Mr. Hynes, who usually lingered like a ghost.

I'd chosen to stay behind after training so I didn't risk entering an empty home and being brought back to *that* night again.

Mum had been staying at work later than usual for a case, which usually caused these fucking taunting flashbacks to resurface.

So, I was the only one left.

Was I supposed to bring it to her?

I stared at it for a moment, debating my options.

She'd always seemed a bit off at the idea of me going closer to her house than I already had, but I couldn't just leave it there.

Sav didn't forget things. She was the kind of girl who colour-coded her notes and probably alphabetised her books.

I told myself I was just being decent. Good guy behavior, right? But my stomach did that stupid twisty thing it always did when it came to this girl.

I grabbed the bag and left.

✦

The neighborhood Sav came from managed to shock me every time.

It wasn't bad exactly, but it wasn't nice either.

I don't know.

I guess I just pictured her coming from a nicer, more put together part of Ridgewood.

I knocked.

For a second, nothing.

Then the door opened a crack.

It wasn't Sav, though.

It was one of the boys I'd seen with her at the game.

"Hi," the boy whispered, cracking the door open just enough for me to see papers and clothes scattered across the house. "Who are you?"

I kneeled down to his level, realising if he was anything like his sister, sudden movement might have sent him retreating. "I'm Archie." I lifted the bag, gesturing to the name etched into it. "Sav left her bag at school."

"Sav?" another voice called, a second boy appearing in the doorway. This one was closer to my age. The one I'd versed from Ophelia, I realised. "So, you're close to her. Who are ya?"

I sighed. "Archie. I'm friends with your sister."

"Friends, huh?" the second boy said, squinting at me like he didn't buy it. To be fair, neither did I.

I shrugged. "Something like that."

The younger kid stepped back after a beat, tugging the door a little wider. "She's in the kitchen. I'll get her."

Before I could say thanks, he vanished, leaving me standing there like some delivery guy no one invited.

Yeah, something was off.

Without thinking, I walked in uninvited.

"You should stay out there," a boy around twelve said from the couch, a frown appearing on his face. "Savvy won't want you inside."

I didn't listen. Just made my way to the kitchen, stepping over baskets of empty washing. Christ, it was like a farm in here. Just without the animals, or… joy.

"Sav?" I called.

"Archie?" She appeared in the doorway of the kitchen, eyes wider than usual. "What are you doing here?"

I lifted up the bag like it explained everything. "You left this."

She quickly snatched it from my hands. "You- I mean- why did you come inside?"

"I felt like I needed to," I said honestly, searching her eyes for the truth. For some sort of explanation. "Did I need to?"

She bit down on her lip, hesitating for a moment. "No, Archie. You didn't need to."

I nodded, trying not to let it sting. But it did.

"Right," I said, taking a step back. "Sorry."

She sighed, like the breath had been knocked out of her. "No. I mean…"

She looked past me, at the boys on the couch, then back to me. Something flickered across her face. Embarrassment, maybe. Or something closer to panic.

"I just don't like people being in my house," she admitted. Her voice was honest, but I had a feeling there was more to the story.

"You don't have to explain anything," I said.

"Yeah, well, I don't exactly get a choice, do I?" she muttered, turning the tap on like it could drown out the conversation.

I stayed quiet. I didn't want her to feel cornered.

A woman entered the kitchen then. With blonde curls and these tired brown eyes, she looked exactly like the boys.

Mother, I assumed.

"Savannah," her mum sighed, pouring herself a glass of water. "Who is this?"

"A friend," Sav answered, never meeting her mum's eyes. "Let it go."

"Savannah, he will be home any-"

"Don't," she whispered, but it sounded more like a warning.

I didn't know who *he* was.

But the way her mum flinched when Savannah said *don't?* Yeah, that told me enough.

Savannah's knuckles were white around the strap of her bag. She still hadn't looked at me again.

Her mum opened her mouth like she was going to argue, but then… didn't. Just turned, walked out of the kitchen, and closed the door behind her. Not a glance spared for any of her children.

What the fuck?

"You should go now," Sav said quietly, like she was defeated. She still didn't meet my eyes.

"Sav-"

"Please, Archie."

I didn't say anything. What could I say? That I wanted to stay? That I hated the way her voice cracked on *please*? That I didn't know what was going on here but I knew it wasn't okay?

I wanted to argue.

I wanted to demand that I stay.

But the pleading, devastated look in her grey eyes told me seeping into this house was a boundary I should never have crossed.

But I'd do it again.

I needed to know she was safe.

"I need to give you my number," I said. "Please. I need to know that you'll text me if you need to."

She blew out a shaky breath before nodding once. "What's your number?"

"I can write it down."

"Photographic memory," she told me, voice gentle again.

Shit. The girl never failed to impress me.

So, I gave her my number.

And I left.

Because I had a big feeling that if I didn't leave? She'd walk away from me. From whatever this was between us.

And it didn't matter how much or how little she could give me. Losing her completely wasn't an option now. It had stopped being an option the moment we met.

Chapter twenty three

June 1st 2004

SAVANNAH

Lately, I found myself here quite often.

Marlee's grave.

Sometimes I was strong enough to speak, and most days, there was just an aching silence. But it was enough. It was my only way of reaching her, wherever she was.

I wasn't sure when I started coming here. It wasn't like I had a reason. Not a clear one, at least. Maybe it was just easier than pretending everything was fine.

Easier than facing the people who expected me to "move on" or "get over it."

But I wasn't sure how to grieve a friend when she was still alive in my head.

No one ever gave me advice on how to live when I knew she never would again.

"I'm not sure if I'm doing this right," I muttered under my breath. My voice cracked, but I didn't care. Who was there to judge?

I rubbed my hand over my face, trying to wipe away the tension. The eternal sadness. The *guilt*.

"Sorry I haven't been here as much," I said, staring down at the headstone, the carved name etched in stone like it would never change. "I really miss you, Mar."

There was no answer, just the sound of the wind and the distant noise of the world moving on. But sometimes, I liked to pretend she was still listening. Maybe that was the part I needed most. That small, foolish belief. That somehow, she *heard* me.

I didn't believe in a God.

But for Marlee's sake, I let myself believe that she was in a better place.

"I'm not sure if I'll ever be okay with this, Marlee," I continued, my voice barely above a whisper. "This whole life thing isn't quite right without you by my side."

A moment of silence. Just one.

"I'm trying, though," I whispered after a beat. "I'm trying."

A single tear slipped down my cheek, but I didn't wipe it away. Maybe for once, I needed it.

To feel something more than the numbness that clung to me like a second skin.

"Izzie really needed you." I sniffled, blinking out the tears. "Needs. She really needs you."

I squeezed my eyes closed.

"Mar?" I called out, spotting her by the bottom row of the auditorium. "I've been looking all over for you."

"I'm sorry," she whispered, offering me a weak smile. "I needed to think."

"Think about what?" I asked, sitting right beside her. "You know you can talk to me, right?"

"Of course." She nodded. "I'll be just fine."

I didn't believe her.

Not really.

But I knew Marlee, and I knew she wanted me to let it go.

"Okay," I said, sliding my hand into hers. "But you're gonna be okay, right?"

She hesitated before nodding. "I'm gonna be just fine, Savvy."

"You don't look fine," I told her carefully.

Her laugh was soft, almost tired. "What does fine even look like?"

"I don't know. Not this."

"I'm just... tired," she admitted, smiling at me. "It'll all be okay in the morning."

She didn't mean she needed sleep.

Fuck, how didn't I see it?

"I love you, you know?" she said, cutting me off before I could even reply. "You're one of my favourite people in the world."

I frowned. "I love you too."

"I should get going," she said eventually, standing too quickly.

"Will you text me tonight?" I asked, panic flickering in my chest.

She nodded. "Of course."

But she didn't.

She never did.

That was the last time I ever saw Marlee.

"Sav?" A voice dragged me away from my memories, dragging me back into reality. Instantly, I could hear the deep voice I'd learned to memorise. "Hi."

"Hi, Archie." I offered a weak smile, not bothering to wipe my tears.

He'd seen the inside of my house, after all.

My only consolation that night was the fact my dad had stormed out a few moments before.

But was it bad that I almost wanted him to see how bad it really was?

It was stupid. I knew that.

But God, I just wanted to be safe. I wanted to know how true safety felt.

"What are you doing here?" I asked, tilting my head to the side.

He gestured vaguely to two graves across the yard. "My dad and Elsie. I come here a lot."

"Me too," I admitted quietly, wiping my eyes with the sleeve of my hoodie. "It's strange, isn't it? Talking to their graves, like they're gonna reply.."

"Yeah," he agreed, joining me at Marlee's. "It feels strange, but it's also kinda… comforting, you know?"

I nodded in understanding, laying a rose on Marlee's grave. My hands lingered there for a moment longer, unwilling to let go of something that felt so final. But it was just a flower. Just a moment.

"Hey, Sav?" he whispered after a few moments of silence. "Your house. It was off."

"Off?" I repeated, alarmed.

He nodded in confirmation. "I don't mean to pry or anything, but I just… It worried me."

"There's nothing to worry about," I lied through my teeth, hoping he would believe me, or at least pretend to.

Archie's eyes were soft with concern, but I refused to let myself break in front of him. Not today. Not when I was already barely holding it together. Not when I was *so* close to telling him things I'd never said before.

"It's just… It gets…" I trailed off, unsure of how to put it into words without sounding like I was asking for pity. Maybe I was. Maybe I wanted someone to see that everything wasn't okay, even if I wasn't ready to admit it.

"Sav, you don't have to explain," he said gently, his voice almost a whisper against the wind. "But if you ever want to talk about it, I'm here."

I offered a half-smile, one that didn't quite meet my eyes. The offer was there, and I knew he meant it, but I wasn't sure if I could take him up on it. Not yet. Maybe not ever. Regardless of how much my heart wanted me to.

Instead, I focused on the small rose I had placed on Marlee's grave. The petals were soft, delicate, yet the thorns were still sharp. Like everything else.

"I should let you have some space," he added quietly, turning to leave.

I didn't want him to go. I wanted him to stay here, wrapped in the silence, in the shared grief. But I knew I couldn't stay forever. And I couldn't beg somebody to stay when my actions said the opposite.

"Thanks, Archie," I said as he began to walk away. He stopped but didn't turn around.

"I'll be seeing you," he said softly, then disappeared into the blur of graves.

I stood there a little longer, letting the wind ruffle my hair and my thoughts. I didn't know what tomorrow would bring. Or the day after. I didn't know how I was going to heal, or if I even would.

But I was here. And somehow, that had to be enough.

Chapter twenty four

June 1st 2004

ARCHIE

"I'm telling you, you're in love with the girl," Theo said drunkenly, an obnoxious grin spreading across his face.

"Shut the fuck up," I warned. "That's not love. It's just… caring."

"Yeah," Theo mocked, rolling his eyes. "And I'm in love with Livvy."

I raised an eyebrow. "You quite literally are."

"I meant the other way around," he slurred. "You love her."

Theo was a dickhead majority of the time, and it was far too soon to even think about love. I *never* wanted to think about love. But he wasn't entirely wrong, either. This was bigger than I thought.

"You don't give me relationship advice," I chuckled, finishing my beer. "You've been after the same girl for years but you're *still* afraid to admit your feelings."

"Am not," he argued, but it was weak, and we both knew it.. "I tell her I'm in love with her every day."

"And you flirt with other girls the next day." I shrugged, clapping a hand on his shoulder. "It won't go anywhere if she doesn't believe you. If you don't *let* her believe you."

He groaned. "What, and you're not hooking up with random girls every week?"

"No," I said honestly. "Not anymore."

"Huh," he breathed, seemingly impressed. "Point in question."

I groaned, opening my mouth to speak, but quickly closing it again when a vaguely familiar face slid into the seat next to me.

Friend?

Enemy?

"Archie Bennett." The blonde boy grinned, snatching my second beer right from my hands. "How are we tonight?"

"Good," I said slowly, raising an eyebrow. "Sorry, who are you?"

"You're in love with my sister," he chuckled, downing the beer in one sip.

"Savannah," Theo filled in with a smirk before turning to me. "He's Savannah's brother."

"Yeah," I deadpanned. "I got that far."

"So," he started, searching me like I was some puzzle with hidden parts. "What are you doing with her?"

"Friends," I muttered, grabbing another beer. "We're friends."

"Right," Theo snorted. "And I'm the pope."

I shot him a warning look, but the fucker didn't care. He was clearly amused.

"We *are* friends," I insisted, looking back at her brother. "And yeah, I plan to stick around."

He leaned back, folding his arms over his chest. Not in some casual, overprotective brother way, either. He was measuring me.

"She doesn't let people in," he explained slowly. "Especially not guys. So either you're lying to yourself… or you're lying to her."

Lying to her? Fuck. This wasn't an easy family to impress.

I gritted my teeth. "That's not exactly fair."

"Maybe," he replied, shrugging. "But she's my sister. She's been through a lot, so I don't give a shit about fair."

I leaned back in my chair without another word, understanding his point. "I'm not going to hurt her."

"Good." He nodded in approval. "Good luck getting all the way in, bud."

"What?" I raised an eyebrow.

"She is not an easy person to know, and she certainly won't change that for the first boy she likes." He glared at me, but it was less confrontational now. "You have to prove your worth sticking around for."

I ran a hand down my face. "Yeah, I'm trying."

"Good." He paused, chuckling to himself after a minute. "I'm Jayden, by the way." He stood, patting me on the shoulder like we were old friends. "Don't screw her over, or I will find you. And I won't hesitate to rip that head off your fucking body."

He walked off without another word, leaving behind the ghost of a warning and an emptier beer bottle.

Theo snorted into his drink. "You're *so* screwed."

I frowned, leaning back in my seat.

Maybe I was.

But I wasn't sure that I cared.

Theo kept watching me like I'd just walked into a trap with my eyes wide open.

"You know what this means, yeah?" Theo grinned.

"That Jayden Grey has boundary issues?" I replied, scoffing.

He chuckled. "Nah. Family's involved now. You don't get threats unless you matter."

I rolled my eyes, downing another beer. "You're thinking about it too much. The guy just loves his sister."

"Am I?" Theo tilted his head. "Because that wasn't a casual 'stay away from my sister' speech. That gave me more of a 'hurt her and I'll bury you in the woods' kinda feeling. Sorry. That's basically what he said," he snickered.

He wasn't wrong.

Jayden and Sav seemed to have quite a close bond. I wasn't sure why or how, because when Elsie had been alive, ninety-nine percent of that time was spent bickering.

But them?

They seemed to rely on each other like lifelines.

I sighed, suddenly standing up. "I need some air."

"You're running away," Theo announced. "Whatever you do, don't run away from her."

"I don't plan on it," I responded.

"You mean something," he called once I was walking away. "She hasn't run yet. Don't let that change."

I stepped outside into the breeze of the night, the music and laughter fading into background noise.

Friends.

That's what I'd said. What I'd intended to happen. And it had started that way. There may have always been something there, but it was easier at the beginning. But somewhere between driving her home and the way her grey eyes looked at me like I wasn't half as fucked up as everybody else thought... something changed.

Something that I wasn't coming back from.

Chapter twenty five

June 5th 2004

SAVANNAH

I'm not sure how I ended up there.

One moment, I was fighting off my dad and keeping my brothers hidden behind the couch.

But the next? I was in Archie's car.

It was stupid, really.

I didn't give him anything more than my usual 'I'm always okay' line, but I still chose him. When things fell apart and I needed someone to lean on, I called *him*.

I'd never called anyone else.

"Are you ever gonna tell me the full story?" he asked, making a sharp turn.

"I don't…" I trailed off. What was I supposed to say?

He was right. I wasn't giving him the whole story. Not even half of it.

Archie sighed, but he didn't push. I think he knew very well how easily I ran.

Not with him though.

I wanted to keep him. All of him.

Always.

God, where did that thought come from?

"I just need to get out sometimes," I said quietly, eyes fixed on the blurry street lights outside the window. "But it's nothing more than that."

"And the bruises?" he continued, jaw flexed. "What about those, Sav? Because you sure as hell fall down the stairs a lot."

I froze, but didn't let it show.

Because I was falling. Trusting.

I wasn't supposed to do that.

I knew I could love him if I allowed myself. If I could only get out of my house.

And God, those were lovely thoughts.

But they were pretend.

Nothing would ever change.

He didn't say anything for a while. Just kept one hand on the wheel, the other resting casually on the gearstick, fingers tapping like he was trying to play it cool. But I saw the way his jaw tensed every time we turned, like he knew what he wanted to say, but he was desperately trying to hold it in.

Eventually, he exhaled a sharp breath and said, "I hate knowing that you're lying."

I didn't respond.

He was right.

It didn't matter how many years I spent building up my walls, they were crumbling down before my eyes. Because of him. *For him.*

"I'm not like everyone else. You're clearly not okay, and I... fuck," he groaned, running a hand down his face, never meeting my eyes. "I want to be the one to help."

I hated how much those few words meant to me. How badly I wanted them to be true.

"I'm not just... I'm not some broken girl you can fix by doing whatever this is," I snapped, my tone coming across as bitter, even to me.

"Do you think that's what I'm doing?" he said gently, his grip on the wheel tightening. "Trying to fix you?"

I didn't answer. Didn't need to.

He pulled the car to a sudden stop, cutting the engine. Silence swallowed us whole, only audible noise being the slight rustle of trees outside. My breath caught in my throat.

"Look at me, Sav."

I didn't.

"Damn it, please. Please look at me Sav," he repeated, and the pleading tone in his voice caused me to tilt my head upward, meeting his eyes.

"I'm not here because I feel sorry for you. I'm not playing the hero. You called me. *You*. I didn't show up out of nowhere," he continued, shaking his head. "So, yeah. Maybe you're not ready to explain the shit going on in your head. Maybe I don't understand. But I am not going anywhere, do you hear me? Not even if you tell me to."

That part scared me most. That he meant it.

"Are you…" he trailed off, squeezing his eyes closed like he was searching for the right words. "Are you safe? At home?"

"Sometimes I am," I heard myself admit quietly, for the first time ever. "Sometimes I'm not."

It was all over his face then. The way something in his eyes sharpened. Darkened. The obvious clench in his jaw.

"I just needed to get out tonight," I said, before whispering, "And I wanted that to be with you."

"Alright," he muttered. "Then we'll just drive."

"Thank you."

So we did.

For a while, we were completely silent.

"I have to get home soon," I finally mumbled a few minutes later, hating how small my voice sounded. "I can't stay out too long."

"It's the weekend," he whispered. "Do you have to go back tonight?"

Back didn't just mean home for me.

It meant back to the man who raised his voice and resorted to fists when life didn't go his way.

"I have to," I whispered back.

"No, you don't," he replied, voice firmer now. "You always stay at Liv's on the weekend."

I swallowed hard, eyes fixed on the road ahead. "This isn't the same thing."

"Why not?" He shrugged, but I could tell this mattered to him. Me. I mattered. "Say you're staying at Liv's."

I tilted my head in curiosity. "And do what?"

He hesitated before saying, "And stay at my house."

Did he just offer for me to sleep over?

At his house?

Savannah, do not say yes!

"Okay," I heard myself agree. "If you're sure?"

"I am very fucking sure." He nodded, exhaling a breath that sounded relieved. "Thank you."

I didn't say anything. Just offered him a tiny smile. The kind that only appeared when I was around him.

"When your house isn't safe," he started carefully. "What happens?"

"Nothing happens," I lied. "I really, really don't want to talk about it."

"That's fine." He turned the corner onto a vaguely familiar street. His street. "But, don't run away from me. Okay?"

I bit down nervously on my lip.

"Please," he whispered, almost begging. "Don't run away."

"I'm still here, aren't I?"

"Yeah." He blew out a shaky breath, pulling into his impressive driveway. "You're still here."

He cut the engine and sat there for a moment, fingers still curled around the keys like he wasn't ready to let go of the night just yet.

I didn't move either. I felt like if I did, something would break. Some fragile piece of this moment that had somehow, impossibly, made me feel safe.

"Come on," he said softly, walking around the car to open my door. "Let's go inside."

The house was completely silent when we stepped inside. It was late, so it made sense. But I had a feeling this house wasn't the same as it used to be.

It must have been different.

Before he lost his family. Lost a part of himself.

Archie flipped on a light, still keeping it low. "Are you hungry or anything?"

"No,' I whispered, glancing around his house. "I don't need anything. Thank you."

He didn't look convinced, but nodded anyway. He started walking toward the stairs, so I followed him up and into his bedroom.

I paused in the doorway, eyes darting around the room. What the hell was I even doing?

"You can take the bed," he said, removing his hoodie and dropping it on his chair. "I'll sleep on the couch."

"Archie, no," I argued. "I'm not kicking you out of your own bed."

He sighed. "You're not kicking me out. I'm telling you."

As he turned to leave, my arm reached out for his sleeve involuntarily. "Can you stay?" I heard myself ask. "Not on the couch or the floor. Just… Can you stay?"

He nodded without hesitation. "Yeah. Yeah, of course."

I slid under the covers, hoping this wasn't too much of an inconvenience.

Archie hopped on the opposite side of his impressively massive bed, keeping a distance between us without staying too far away.

I'd literally just asked him to stay.

With me.

In bed.

Yeah, I was losing my head.

"Are you okay?" He asked from beside me, voice soft.

I smiled. "I'm wonderful."

"That you are, Savannah Grey," he sighed, eyes closing. "That you are."

I rolled onto my side, closing my eyes.

And for the first time since I was born, I wasn't afraid of the darkness or silence.

Because I was no longer alone in it.

Chapter twenty six
June 10th 2004

ARCHIE

I wasn't supposed to be in her class.

Honestly, she was a whole lot smarter than me and I was supposed to be in the class below, but I couldn't fucking stay away.

The girl was killing me, and I think I'd been in love with her since the first time we spoke.

"Archie?" Sav whispered from the desk beside mine, tilting her head to the side. "You take law?"

I sighed, debating whether I was supposed to tell her I'd sat in simply to watch her. Yeah, no. Slightly too creepy.

I shrugged. "Needed a change."

Half-truth.

Because I did need a change.

But she was the change that I needed.

"Oh, okay." She offered me a smile, one that seemed genuine. "I'm glad."

I grinned despite myself. "Are ya?"

"Mm hm," she laughed softly, scribbling something down in her notebook. "Mr. Lantz is always late, and the school said we can leave next time he takes longer than ten minutes."

Chuckling, I asked, "how long has it been?"

Her grey eyes flickered up to the clock, smiling to herself. "Nine minutes."

"You're quite happy about that," I stated, frowning. "Why do you take law if you don't like it?"

She hesitated. "I do like it. I love it. But it's never going to lead anywhere."

That spiked my interest. Or my concern. "Why not? You're clearly good at it."

She sighed, shrugging. "It's not that easy."

She said it like it fucking hurt, but I decided not to ask any more questions. She was so close. So bloody close to letting me in entirely. I couldn't risk losing that now.

"Ten minutes," I whispered once the clock hit eleven. "Wanna get out of here?"

"With you?" She asked.

I laughed. "With me, Sav," I confirmed, hopeful.

"Okay," she said without hesitation, rising from her chair. "Let's go."

We slipped out of the classroom almost immediately, her hand brushing against mine for a moment too long. I didn't say anything. I didn't need to. I could feel it all the same.

The air outside was thick, the blue sky replaced by grey clouds. By the time we made it out of the gates, I felt the first splash of rain against my cheek.

We walked in silence for a few minutes before I slid one of my headphones from my ear, and held it out for her without a word. She took it almost instantly, accidentally brushing against my shoulder as she placed it in her ear.

Coldplay's *Iris* was already playing. I'd had it on repeat for the last week. Every lyric reminded me of *her.*

She looked at me, a smile playing on her lips. "You like this song."

I nodded, glancing sideways at her. "Do you?"

Her smile appeared fully as she whispered, "Yeah."

The corners of my mouth tugged upward involuntarily. Her voice was quiet, like the song was a secret just between us now.

We didn't need to speak after that.

The rain picked up as we made our way to the nearby park, causing raindrops to land on her long lashes. Christ, she was always beautiful, but now… she was unreal. She looked like something straight out of a movie.

Someone you never really stop wanting.

"God, it's freezing." The rain started pouring, and she threw her head back in laughter as I spun her around.

"It is," I agreed, unable to hide my endless joy. "You're beautiful," I said before I could stop myself.

Fuck, she was.

So beautiful it hurt.

Her laughter quickly slowed as she looked up at me with those wide, grey eyes that had turned from guarded to trusting in a few months' time.

God, how much that meant.

"Archie," she breathed, gazing into my eyes like this was the first time she saw me. Really saw me.

I didn't say anything. I just looked down at her, never breaking our gaze.

I couldn't risk it.

If I said anything, if I moved even a centimetre, I could ruin this completely. Shatter it. And Christ, the girl was too important to me now.

"Is this…" She hesitated, staring into my eyes like she was calculating something. "Is this the part where you kiss me?" She asked softly, attention flicking from my eyes to my lips.

I froze, but quickly regained my composure. "Do you want this to be the part where I kiss you?" I replied, voice raising just enough for her to hear me over the rain.

"I think so," she answered, voice honest and… happy. She sounded *happy.* "Yeah. Yeah, I want this to be the part where you kiss me."

I swallowed hard, eyes fixed on her lips now.

And God, those lips.

The lips I'd been dreaming of for longer than I cared to admit.

I leaned in slowly, and the world seemed to fade away. It was as if we were the only two people on the planet.

And, if so? I was a very lucky one.

Her breath caught, and I felt it. The moment before our lips touched, her hand reached out to hold mine.

And that's when I knew.

That's when I knew.

Not the kiss. Not even her words. But the fact that she reached for my hand. Trusting me with that. Choosing me in that second.

My lips brushed hers, soft and tender, and I could feel her smile against my lips before I pulled her a little closer, deepening the kiss just enough. My hands slid down to her waist, gentle and fucking trembling.

God, this girl.

This. Girl.

The rain fell heavier around us, but I swear, I barely noticed. Her hands slid to my shoulders, and I let my forehead rest against hers when we broke apart, breathless and grinning like idiots.

"Thanks," she whispered, pulling her head back slightly.

"For kissing you?" I laughed softly, my hand still resting on her cheek. "I think I should be thanking you."

"No." She shook her head, eyes full of something deep. Hope? I wasn't sure. "For staying."

"I told you," I whispered. "I told you I wasn't going anywhere."

"You might," she muttered beneath her breath, like maybe it was just meant for her. But I heard it.

"No, I won't."

"It might get messy, and you might not understand," she said, not making any sense. "But I owe you everything. Because knowing you kept me afloat like nothing else."

I smiled again, hand never leaving her face.

"But I do have to go home," she told me, frowning slightly. "You know I have to go home."

"I know," I sighed. "But I really don't like that."

"Why?" She asked, eyes widening.

"Because I don't think you're giving me the full story," I admitted honestly.

"One day." She nodded, more to herself than me. She wanted to believe it, I could see that.

All I could hope was for it to be true.

She bit down nervously on her lip before taking a few steps back, smiling as she did. "You're a wonderful kisser, Archie Bennett," she giggled.

With that, she was gone.

Chapter twenty seven
June 12th 2004

SAVANNAH

It had been two days since Archie kissed me.

While two days sounded short, it wasn't. God, it wasn't. Because those two days were filled with emotions. Like, every one in the book.

I wanted him to kiss me.

I did.

But there was still so much unresolved baggage.

No matter how hard he tried to brush it off, I knew he wasn't over the death of his father and little sister. I sure as hell wasn't over the death of Marlee, and then… there was the fact that my life had been spent within the walls of violence.

I felt that if I let him in further, if I kept kissing him, things would only go downhill.

Because not everybody gets their happy endings.

"You have to text him." Izzie dragged me back into the present, rolling her eyes.

"Why?" I asked, cheeks flushed.

"Because you like him," she explained. "And he likes you. And you slept in his bed."

Josie's head snapped up. "What?"

"She makes it sound so much worse than it was," I quickly defended. "I was having a rough night. He was nice."

Yeah, I was really bloody screwed.

I thought I'd been hiding my twisted feelings for Archie quite well, but this hang out with my friends told me I was entirely wrong,

I was pretty sure they'd known longer than me.

But they didn't know about the kiss.

"What am I supposed to say?" I asked, completely uneducated when it came to boys.

Liv giggled. "Just *text* him. It doesn't need to be anything crazy."

I frowned. "This doesn't happen to me."

"Feelings?' Josie asked, tilting her head. "We all thought that at some point. But I knew it would happen for you this year."

"You were betting on my romantic life?" I raised an eyebrow. "You're a strange one."

"Well, that boy has been watching you for years." Josie shrugged, brushing back a strand of auburn hair. "Sure, he spent the past few years hooking up with random girls and-"

I scrunched my nose up.

"Right, sorry," Josie laughed. "You know what I mean. He hasn't even seen another girl since the first time you guys properly spoke."

"How do you know that?" I questioned, sounding far too curious.

"I have connections." Josie wiggled her eyebrows.

"It's true," Liv chimed in then.

I didn't get it.

I'd given him close to nothing.

Seriously, I didn't know what he saw in me.

I didn't have very much to offer.

"Stop worrying." Liv offered me a genuine smile. "I know this is big for you."

"Yeah," I agreed.

This was big for me.

I was realising just how deep I was now. There was no turning back.

I liked him. I mean, I really, really liked him. This was bad.

Or amazing.

Ugh.

"Text him," Izzie repeated, passing me my phone. "Or I will."

"You would not," Josie said.

"She absolutely would." I nodded slowly, taking my phone. "Seriously, I don't know what to say!"

'Say hi," Liv laughed like it was the stupidest question in the world.

Was I supposed to text him?

I hadn't spoken to him since the kiss. The time I felt safer than ever before.

I wished I had more to offer. More to give.

But the least I could do was message him. Let him know I didn't forget about him.

Not that that was possible.

"I kissed him," I heard myself admit in a murmur.

"What?" Josie's eyes widened, lips turning into a grin. "Oh my God!"

Liv's mouth opened slightly, but quickly closed. "We're surprised… why?"

"It was bound to happen," Izzie hummed. "Good girl."

"Okay. Okay. That just means you definitely have to text him! He was at the gym with Theo," Liv explained. "It's the perfect time to message."

So, I did exactly that.

I simply messaged him:

Hey.

I stared at the screen for a moment before my friends huddled around my phone like we were in some sort of secret meeting.

"That's it?" Josie asked, frowning.

"It's safe," I defended, clutching my phone.

"It's boring," Izzie groaned, but there was a smile on her face.

"It is safe." Liv shrugged. "Safe is fine."

My phone buzzed, and all of us jumped.

Archie:
Hey. Didn't forget about me?

My heart did something weird. Like a hiccup and a flip all at once.

"God, he absolutely wants to be with you," Izzie said, reading the text. "Let go of the fear."

I bit down on my lip. Of course I hadn't forgotten about him. I'd thought about him every second of every damn day. And that wasn't so scary now.

Me: *I didn't forget. I just didn't know what to say.*

Archie: *You don't need to say anything. I'll be here when you're ready.*

I blinked at the screen.

"I think I'm ready," I whispered before I could stop myself.

I was. Maybe.

Nothing had changed. Not really. But I had.

I couldn't keep waiting for something to change just so I could find happiness. I needed to *be* the change.

Josie's head whipped toward me. "What?"

"I think... I want to see him," I blurted out. "Like now."

Liv beamed, eyes widening. "Then be brave! Ask him."

I hesitated for a moment before typing a message. But I had no time to send it before another one came through. From him.

Archie: *Are you free tonight?*
Me: Yeah. I'm at Liv's.
Archie: *Wanna go to Romano's?*

My finger hovered slightly over the screen.

He just asked me out.

Did he mean it as a date?

Me: *I'd love to.*

✦

The restaurant was dimly lit, fairy lights pinned across the walls.

It was surprisingly quiet. The sort of place you'd only find if you knew about it, tucked between a florist and park.

"You look beautiful, if I didn't say that already," Archie said casually, sipping his water slowly.

"Thanks." I smiled slightly. "Is… um, is this a date?" I blurted out before I could stop myself.

"This can be whatever you want it to be," Archie assured me with a small chuckle. "And I can be anyone you want me to be."

I swallowed hard, my eyes fixed on the steak in front of me. I felt guilty eating it. Making him pay.

"Are you sure about this? I just… I can't pay you back," I admitted.

He grinned, pushing the plate closer to me. "Even if this isn't a date, I never planned to make you pay."

"Thank you," I whispered, but we both knew it wasn't about the money or the food. It was about the fact he'd been my first safe place. Somewhere along the line, he became my person.

"Always." He nodded. "You know that."

"Yeah," I agreed. "I do."

Archie smiled, but it wasn't one of those cocky, smug ones he wore at parties. This was one of the soft, genuine ones he only wore when it was the two of us.

He leaned back slightly, his fingers brushing the edge of his water glass. "You don't have to explain anything to me, Sav. I'll be honest, your life is a mystery I cannot begin to figure out. But I'm not going anywhere. I'm here to stay."

I blinked, words sinking in. "Why?"

"You're worth waiting for," he replied without a hint of hesitation. "Very worth it."

There was a pause. A beat of silence.

I didn't know what to say to that.

So I looked at him.

Archie Bennett, against all odds, had been the boy to give me hope and catch me when I fell. And somehow, miraculously, he didn't walk away.

Neither did I.

"I'm scared," I whispered, finally admitting it aloud.

"I know."

"And I don't have it all figured out."

"I know."

"And I can't walk away," I added, voice barely above a whisper. "I'm always halfway out the door. But with you? I'm so inside the door that I'm losing my mind," I paused mid-ramble, noticing his dark green eyes watching me right back.

"Good." He nodded. "Because I'd like you to stick around. Very much."

I smiled despite myself.

Maybe I needed to give in.

To take a breath and finally let myself live.

Or maybe I wouldn't escape this pattern of sadness until the very end.

"I want to be with you, Sav," he confessed, voice barely above a whisper. "I think that's been clear since the very beginning."

I swallowed hard, eyes fixed on the plate in front of me.

I knew that.

I knew he wanted to be with me. And even though it confused the hell out of me, I wanted to be with him as well.

But it was easier said than done.

"Archie," I tried, but he shook his head to silence me.

"I'm not saying it has to be now," he murmured, choosing his words carefully like he was afraid of breaking this weird, fragile thing between us. "And I'm not saying you have to want me either. But I'm telling you what I want. What I want… is you."

I bit down on my lip, completely at a loss for words.

What did he want me to say?

There were no words in the English language that could explain this. To me. To him.

"Tell me the truth, Sav." He stared into my eyes, silently pleading. "What is it? Why are you so afraid?"

Because my father would kill me.

He would kill both of us.

"You scare me, okay?" I whispered, half-honest. "You terrify me."

His green eyes widened in realisation. "I scare you? Why?"

I shook my head, realising the weight of my own words. "Not in a way that I believe you'd ever hurt me, but in a way that... I don't know. I'd let you in," I hurried to clarify. "I'd let you in more than I already have."

He listened intently, eyes never leaving mine. "And what if I promise not to hurt you? What if I promise to be there, to listen?"

My gaze dropped to the floor. "That might be even scarier."

A flash of sadness appeared in his eyes. "Why is it so scary to trust someone?"

"How is it not?" I asked in a whisper, finally being honest with him.

He looked at me like I was a puzzle trying to complete, but he was still missing the corners. "It's not me you're scared of."

With no fight left in me, I simply shrugged. "Sav?"

"It's not that simple," I heard myself murmur.

"Then explain it to me," he urged, concern visibly growing. "God, help me understand because I'm losing my mind a little bit here."

I looked away, the pain of the things I'd been carrying my whole life weighing down on me like a brick.

"Please," he said, his voice almost pleading. "It's like there's a really tall wall between us. In front of you. I don't know if I'm supposed to keep climbing it or just wait, and hope that maybe one day, you'll open the door."

"I'm trying," I whispered honestly. "But you don't know what sort of life you're asking for a key into."

"I don't care." He threw his hands up helplessly. "You could stick a knife in my throat, Sav, and I still wouldn't regret knowing you."

I frowned. "You're very persistent."

"Very." A smile played on his lips, usual demeanor returning. "And I've never been more persistent about anything."

Chapter twenty eight

June 15th 2004

ARCHIE

For the first time in sixteen years, training felt pointless.

Because of her.

Everything was because of *her*.

She did want to be with me. We kissed. And in her own, small way, she admitted it.

My mind was entirely occupied by the girl.

The way her small hands brushed against mine, the way her eyes lingered on mine like she was searching for something she was afraid to find.

And just like that, sixteen years of purpose, of discipline were undone in a breath.

What was I even fighting anymore?

She had her own demons. I saw that. I knew that the very first day.

I didn't go into this blind.

But I still couldn't figure out what the fuck was going on in that head of hers.

"Archie," Theo called, jogging over to me. "Are you coming on the weekend?"

"Where?" I asked, throwing the ball right through the hoop.

"Livvy's 16th is on the weekend," he explained with that obnoxious fucking grin he always wore. "We're going camping."

"Doesn't she hate camping?" I raised an eyebrow.

"No." He rolled his eyes. "The rest of them do. Livvy and... Marlee always loved it."

I nodded.

"Sav's going."

"Yeah, I'll be there," I said immediately, hating how desperate I sounded.

Theo's grin stretched wider, but he didn't call me on it. Just clapped me on the shoulder like we were still twelve and none of this had gotten complicated yet. "Good. I'll text ya later," he announced, already chatting to another guy on the court.

I stood there for a second, ball still in my hands, heart punching against my ribs like I'd just sprinted a marathon.

Sav was going.

Of course she was.

This wasn't over.

Not by a long shot.

And maybe I was a fool for thinking one weekend would change anything. But I *had* to try.

I took another shot. Missed.

First time in months.

Didn't even care.

Because Savannah Grey could unravel me without even trying. Maybe she knew. Maybe she didn't. It didn't bloody matter.

She had some sort of power or control over me. It was fucking strange, but it was there.

I always felt like she was two steps away from letting me in. She'd lean in, then slam the door like she was afraid of what I might find.

But there was nobody else for me. I needed her to know that.

A year ago, hell, a month ago, I would have laughed at that comment. But the girl was screwing with my head. Had been since February.

I never wanted kids.

That was a hard no.

But with her?

I could be a good father.

Shit. Those thoughts didn't belong in my mind.

Yeah, she was screwing with my head for sure.

The weekend couldn't come fast enough.

Not because I believed it would change anything, because I meant it when I told her I'd wait. I would wait years if it meant I could have her.

I just wanted to be near her.

To see if there was a part of her, even the smallest part, that was willing to *try*.

And yeah, I wanted to kiss her again, but fuck, I just needed her to know I was serious about this.

About *her.*

Because somehow, I was.

She mattered more than anything else ever had, and that was fucking terrifying.

I walked off the court, sweat sticking to my skin, but my blood ran cold.

There were a hundred reasons I shouldn't go.

And only one reason I would.

Her.

Chapter twenty nine
June 19th 2004

SAVANNAH

"Happy birthday," I exclaimed, sliding into Archie's familiar car. I passed Liv a card containing 30 dollars, courtesy of Jayden, smiling slightly. "I'm sorry it's not much."

"Oh, shush," Liv giggled sweetly, poking my arm. "I'm just happy you're here."

I exhaled a relieved breath, buckling my seatbelt.

Somehow, it took me a good ten minutes on the road to realise who I was sitting next to.

That, of course, was Archie.

"Oh! Hi," I said, smiling. "I didn't see you."

He chuckled, nudging my shoulder. "I saw you."

I swallowed, turning my attention back to Liv and Theo in the front. "So, what's the plan for tonight?" I asked, desperate to steer the conversation to neutral ground.

"Camping, but fun," Theo said simply.

"That means he brought microphones," Billy groaned from the far back. "The glitter ones."

"Hey," Theo warned. "They were the best ones in the shop."

"You needed microphones... why?" Danny asked, tilting his head.

Theo scoffed like that was a completely unbelievable question. "To *sing*."

Liv shook her head. "Anyway, it'll be fun!"

I smiled to myself, enjoying the chaos. Because I was finally with the people I loved, not the ones I feared.

It was lovely.

"Are we really doing karaoke in the woods?" I asked, half-laughing at the absurdity of it all.

"Of course we are," Liv said, grinning mischievously. "Why not? I mean, what's camping without a little... extra?"

Billy groaned again. "Every time I'm with you fuckers, I wonder why I came."

"Come on," Archie said between chuckles. You're not going to get away from it, might as well embrace it."

Izzie sighed from the back seat, speaking up for the first time today. "What are the tent arrangements?"

"You think I planned that far?" Theo raised a brow.

"No," Izzie said, pointing a finger at Liv. "I think she did."

Theo sighed, tilting his head to look at Liv, still keeping both hands on the wheel. "Did you go Livvy-planny mode?"

"I did." Liv nodded proudly. "And, no. You're not sharing a tent with me."

"Even if I say please?"

"No, Theodore." Liv shook her head, glancing down at the notebook in her hands. "Because that would put Archie and Savannah… hm." She paused, looking at me with that mischievous grin.

"What?" I asked, cheeks slightly flushed.

"Savannah, do ya mind sharing a tent with Archie?" Theo asked from the front. "I need alone time with the love of my life."

"Would you shut up?" Liv groaned, glancing at me again. Her gaze was almost pleading.

She wanted to be with Theo, I realised.

And it was her birthday. So…

"I'm okay with that," I said, keeping my gaze on the floor.

Liv shot me a grateful smile, her eyes lighting up with relief. "Thanks, Savannah."

I tried not to make a big deal out of it. It was just one night, just a tent, and it wasn't like I didn't enjoy Archie's company. It was that I enjoyed it too much.

But again, it was one night.

I could do that.

For Liv.

"So," I said, forcing my tone to stay casual as I turned toward Archie. "Are you, uh, good with the tent thing?"

He turned his head toward me with a small grin. "Course I am."

I nodded, pretending to focus on the trees whipping past the window. It wasn't like it was a big deal. It was just camping. In a tent. With Archie. Nothing strange about that.

Except, everything was strange.

The campsite came into view then, and it felt like a weight had been lifted from my shoulders.

Not because we were camping. I hated camping. There were bears and spiders and… lots of spine-shivering animals. But because I was at home with these people. They were *my* home.

Theo's voice cut through my thoughts, pulling my attention back to the front. "Alright, let's set up camp. We'll do karaoke after we get everything sorted, so don't go getting too comfortable in your tents."

"Isn't that the whole point of camping?" Josie called from the back, frowning. "Drinking, getting comfy, then regretting it when you wake up with a sore back and pounding head the next day?"

"Don't knock it till you try it," Liv laughed, flinging her door open. "You'll all love it."

I couldn't argue with her there. Again, I was not much of a nature enthusiast. But the idea of lying under the open sky, surrounded by friends, felt appealing in a way I hadn't expected.

Theo opened his door then, turning to face us with a smirk. "Who wants to help set up tents?"

Liv was already out of the car, stretching her arms above her head with a content sigh. "I'm in. Let's get this party started."

I slid out of the car next, and as I did, I caught Archie's eyes. He gave me a small, almost reassuring smile, and I couldn't help but return it.

Maybe tonight wouldn't be as hard as I thought. Maybe it would. Who knew? Either way, I was happy to be here, surrounded by friends.

As the others started unloading the car, I grabbed a few camping supplies, trying to push aside the tiny knot of anxiety in my stomach. It was just one night. Just one night with Archie in a tent.

I could handle it. Right?

✦

"How are you doing?" Archie leaned in to whisper, the rest of the group dancing and swapping microphones carelessly. "I mean, how are you *really* doing?"

I looked at him. "I'm okay." And for the first time in forever, I wholeheartedly meant it.

Maybe it was the alcohol seeping in my system or the fact that I was falling hard and fast for the boy beside me, but I felt good.

I didn't care about much else.

For the first time in years, my fathers voice wasn't ringing in my head, and I wasn't haunted by my brothers' sobs.

I wasn't *absent.*

"You're not lying?" He tilted his head, searching my eyes.

I chuckled. "No. I'm not lying."

He grinned happily. "You're very drunk, though."

I nodded in agreement.

"Hey, Archie?" I half-whispered, half-slurred, squinting at him. "Can I tell you a secret?"

"Anything," he whispered back.

"Do you want to know why my house is bad sometimes?" I heard myself ask.

"Sav." He shook his head, eyes widening slightly. "I don't want you to tell me anything while you're drunk. You'll run away from me tomorrow."

"I won't," I argued. "And my dad gets angry."

"He gets angry?" Archie asked, confused. "How angry, Sav?"

"Violent," I whispered. "He gets violent."

The words slipped out before I could stop them, and the weight of them felt heavy in the air between us. But I was too drunk to care.

"You don't have to say more right now," he said softly, voice gentle but firm. "Don't say more right now. Please. We are both drunk and I can't... fuck, Sav. I can't mess this up with you."

I swallowed, feeling a knot form in my throat. I wasn't meant to say that. Certainly not tonight, and not to him. But the alcohol was clouding my judgment.

I pulled away slightly, shifting in my seat, trying to clear my head. "I'm sorry," I mumbled, avoiding his gaze.

"No," Archie said quickly, reaching for my hand, his grip warm and steady. "It's okay. Don't apologise. I just can't know this stuff and not remember it the next day. But don't think I'll be dropping this tomorrow."

I nodded slowly. "Can we go to the tent?"

"Of course." He smiled, grip tightening on my hand. "Let's go."

We made our way to the tent in silence, my body suddenly hyper-aware of just how close he was. I could feel his hand wrapped around mine, warm and reassuring. His grip was gentle, but it was a constant reminder that he was here, that he wasn't going anywhere.

And God, I didn't want him to.

We zipped the tent, shutting the rest of the chaos out. It was just us. Me and him.

Archie sat across from me then, his eyes studying me softly.

I crawled over to the sleeping bags, sitting down on one and pulling my knees up to my chest, feeling an unexpected vulnerability wash over me.

I wanted him to know, I realised.

It could have been the alcohol, but it felt like more.

He would believe me. He could help. I could be safe.

God, I wanted to be safe.

"Stop worrying," he said, half smiling. "You're fine."

"Thank you," I whispered, my voice barely audible.

He nodded, his gaze soft but unwavering. "You don't have to thank me. I care about you, Sav."

Silence.

"More than I should."

When I looked up, Archie was watching me with that same intensity, his eyes searching mine like he was trying to figure out what I needed, what I wanted. There was a pause, just a breath, and then I couldn't stop myself.

I leaned in, closing the gap between us, and kissed him.

He kissed me back, his hand gently cupping the side of my face, guiding me closer. His touch was tender, as though he was afraid of breaking me, of pushing me too far too fast. But I didn't want him to hold back. I didn't want any more walls between us.

I deepened the kiss, moving impossibly closer. I couldn't lose this. Him. I couldn't.

I could lose anything else. But not him.

Not. Him.

When we finally pulled away, both of us breathless, I couldn't help but smile, my heart racing in a way I'd only ever felt after our first kiss.

Yeah, this was my second kiss ever.

Both of which were with him.

And both were very bloody good.

"I'm… uh…" I stuttered, never breaking our gaze.

He chuckled, his thumb gently rubbing my cheek. "Don't worry. Don't ever worry again."

I smiled, and in that moment, I felt at peace.

Maybe everything would be okay now.

I could figure it out.

But I was wrong.

My phone rang, and I declined it the first few times, desperate to stay in this moment forever.

But on the fourth ring, when I saw Jayden's name, I realised I couldn't ignore it any longer.

The boys might need me.

"Hello?" I said, answering the call. "Jay, is everything okay?"

Jayden didn't answer, and that scared me more. "Jay."

Archie's hand never left my cheek as he glanced at me, clearly as worried as I was.

"Jay?" I repeated, alarm growing. "Please tell me. What happened?"

I heard him let out a breath on the other end, one that sounded painful. He was *crying*, I realised.

"There was an accident."

www.ingramcontent.com/pod-product-compliance
Lightning Source LLC
Chambersburg PA
CBHW022147170626
46807CB00005B/2106